REBIRTH

BOOK 1 OF THE PRAEGRESSUS PROJECT

AARON HODGES

Written by Aaron Hodges
Edited by M. M. Chabot
Proofread by Tee Ayer and Sara Pinnell
Cover Art by Christian Bentulan

The Praegressus Project
Book 1: Rebirth
Book 2: Renegades
Book 3: Retaliation
Book 4: Rebellion
Book 5: Retribution

The Sword of Light Trilogy
Book 1: Stormwielder
Book 2: Firestorm
Book 3: Soul Blade

Aaron Hodges was born in 1989 in the small town of Whakatane, New Zealand. He studied for five years at the University of Auckland, completing a Bachelor's of Science in Biology and Geography, and a Masters of Environmental Engineering. After working as an environmental consultant for two years, he grew tired of office work and decided to quit his job and explore the world. During his travels he picked up an old draft of a novel he once wrote in High School – titled The Sword of Light – and began to rewrite the story. Six months later he published his first novel, Stormwielder. And the rest, as they say, is history.

FOLLOW AARON HODGES:
And receive a free short story…

Newsletter:
www.aaronhodges.co.nz/newsletter-signup/

Facebook:
www.facebook.com/Aaron-Hodges-669480156486208/

Bookbub:
www.bookbub.com/authors/aaron-hodges

For the child inside us all.
Let them soar.

ANGELA FALLOW SQUINTED through the rain-streaked windshield, struggling to make out details in the lengthening gloom. A few minutes ago the streetlights had flickered into life, but despite their yellowed light, shadows still hung around the house across the street. Tall hedges marked the boundary with the neighbouring properties, while a white picket fence stood between her car and the old cottage.

Leaning closer to the window, Angela held her breath to keep the glass from fogging, and willed her eyes to pierce the twilight. But beyond the brightly-lit sidewalk, there was no sign of movement. Letting out a long sigh, she sat back in her seat and smiled with quiet satisfaction. There was no sign of anyone outside the house, no silent shadows slipping closer to the warm light streaming from the windows.

At least, none that could be seen.

Berating herself for her nerves, Angela turned her

attention to the touchscreen on her dashboard. Its soft glow brightened as she tapped its screen, making her glad for the tinted windows. No one in the house would be able to see the car was occupied.

Angela pursed her lips, studying the charts on the screen one last time. It displayed the driver's license of a young woman in her early forties. Auburn hair hung around her shoulders and she wore the faintest hint of a smile on her red lips. The smile spread to her cheeks, crinkling the skin around her olive-green eyes.

Margaret Sanders

Beneath the picture was a description of the woman: her height, weight, license number, last known address, school and work history, her current occupation as a college teacher, and marital status. The last was listed as widowed with a single child. Her husband had succumbed to cancer almost a decade previously.

Shaking her head, Angela looked again at the woman's eyes, wondering what could have driven her to this end. She had a house, a son, solid employment as a teacher. Why would she throw it all away, when she had so much to lose?

Idly, she wondered whether Mrs Sanders would have done things differently if given another chance. The smile lines around her eyes were those of a kind soul, and her alleged support for the resistance fighters seemed out of character. It was a shame the government did not give second chances – especially not with traitors of the state.

Now both mother and son would suffer for her actions.

Tapping the screen, Angela pulled up the son's file. Christopher Sanders, at eighteen, was the reason she had come tonight. The assault team would handle the mother and any of her associates who might be on the property, but the son had been selected for the Praegressus project. That meant he had to be taken alive and unharmed.

His profile described him as five-foot-eleven, with a weight of 150 pounds – not large by any measure. Her only concern was the black belt listed beneath his credentials, though Angela knew such accomplishments usually meant little in reality. Particularly when the target was unarmed, unsuspecting and outnumbered.

A picture of her target popped onto the screen with another tap, and a flicker of discomfort spread through her stomach. His brunette hair showed traces of his mother's auburn locks, while the hazel eyes must have descended from a dominant *bey2* allele in his father's chromosome. A hint of light-brown facial hair traced the edges of his jaw, mingling with the last traces of teenage acne. Despite his small size, he had the broad, muscular shoulders of an athlete, and there was little sign of fat on his youthful face.

Sucking in a breath, Angela flicked off the screen. This was not her first assignment, though she hoped it might be her last. For months now she had overseen the collection of subjects for the Praegressus project, and the task had never gotten easier. The faces of the children she had taken haunted her, staring at her when she closed her eyes. Her only consolation was that without her, those children would have suffered the same fate as their parents. At least the research facility gave them a fighting chance.

And looking into the boy's eyes, she knew he was a fighter.

Angela closed her eyes, shoving aside her doubt, and reached out and pressed a button on the car's console.

"Are you in position?" she spoke to the empty car.

"Ready when you are, Fallow," a man replied.

Nodding her head, Fallow reached beneath her seat and retrieved a steel briefcase. Unclipping its restraints, she lifted out a jet injector and held it up to the light. The stainless-steel instrument appeared more like a gun than a piece of medical equipment, but it served its purpose well enough. Once her team had Chris restrained, it would be a simple matter to use the jet injector to anesthetise the young man for transport.

Removing a vial of etorphine from the case, she screwed it into place and pressed a button on the side. A short *hiss* confirmed it was pressurised. She eyed the clear liquid, hoping the details in the boy's file were correct. She had prepared the dosage of etorphine earlier for Chris's age and weight, but a miscalculation could prove fatal.

"Fallow, still waiting on your signal?" the voice came again.

Fallow bit her lip and closed her eyes. Taking a deep breath, she shivered in the cold of the car.

If not you, then someone else.

She opened her eyes. "Go."

CHAPTER 1

CHRIS LET out a long sigh as he settled into the worn-out sofa and then cursed as a broken spring stabbed at his backside. Wriggling sideways to avoid it, he leaned back and reached for the remote, only to realise it had been left beside the television. Muttering under his breath, he climbed back to his feet, retrieved the remote and flicked on the television, then collapsed back into the chair. This time he was careful to avoid the broken springs.

He closed his eyes as the blue glow of the television lit the room. The shriek of the adverts quickly followed, but he barely had the energy to be annoyed. He was still studying full-time, but now his afternoons were taken up by long hours at the construction site. Even then, they were struggling. His only hope was winning a place at the California State University. Otherwise, he would have little choice but to accept the apprenticeship his supervisor was offering.

"Another attack was reported today from the rural

town of Julian," a reporter's voice broke through the stream of adverts, announcing the start of the six o'clock news.

Chris's ears perked up and he opened his eyes to look at the television. Images flashed across the screen of an old mining town, its dusty dirt roads and rundown buildings looking like they had not been touched since the 1900s. A row of horse-drawn carriages lined the street, their owners standing beside them.

The sight was a common one in the rural counties of the Western Allied States. In the thirty years since the states of California, Oregon and Washington had declared their independence, the divide between urban and rural communities had grown exponentially. Today there were few citizens in the countryside who could afford luxuries such as cars and televisions.

"We're just receiving word the police have arrived on the scene," the reporter continued.

On the television, a black van with the letters SWAT painted on the side had just pulled up. The rear doors swung open, and a squad of black-garbed riot-police leapt out. They gathered around the van and then moved on past the carriages. Dust swirled around them, but they moved without hesitation, the camera following them at a distance.

The image changed as the police moved around a corner into an empty street. The new camera angle looked down at the police from the rooftop of a nearby building. It followed the SWAT unit as they split into two groups and spread out along the street, moving quickly, their rifles at the ready.

Then the camera panned down the street and refocused on the broken window of a grocery store. The image grew as the camera zoomed, revealing the nightmare inside the store.

Chris swallowed as images straight from a horror movie flashed across the screen. The remnants of the store lay scattered across the linoleum floor, the contents of broken cans and bottles staining the ground red. Amongst the wreckage, a dozen people lay motionless, face down in the dark red liquid.

The camera tilted and zoomed again, bringing the figures into sharper focus. Chris's stomach twisted and he forced himself to look away. But even the brief glimpse had been enough to see the people in the store were dead. Their pale faces stared blankly into space, the blood drained away, their skin marked by jagged streaks of red and patches of purple. Few, if any of the victims were whole. Pieces of humanity lay scattered across the floor, the broken limbs still dripping blood.

Finally turning back to the television, Chris swallowed as the camera panned in on the sole survivor of the carnage. The man stood amidst the wreckage of the store, blood streaking his face and arms, stained his shirt red. His head was bowed, and the only sign of life was the rhythmic rise and fall of his shoulders. As the camera zoomed on his face, his cold grey eyes were revealed. They stared at the ground, blank and lifeless.

Standing, Chris looked away, struggling to contain the meagre contents of his stomach.

"The *Chead* is thought to have awakened around sixteen hundred hours," the reporter started to speak again, drawing Chris back to the screen. "Special forces have cleared the immediate area and are now preparing to engage with the creature."

"Two hours." Chris jumped as a woman's voice came from behind him.

Spinning on his heel, he let out a long breath as his mother walked in from the kitchen. "I thought you had a night class!" he gasped, his heart racing.

His mother shook her head, a slight smile touching her face. "We finished early." She shrugged, then waved at the television. "They've been standing around for two hours. Watching that thing. Some of those people were still alive when it all started. They could have been saved. Would have, if they'd been somebody important."

Chris pulled himself off the couch and moved across to embrace his mother. Wrapping his arms around her, he kissed her cheek. She returned the gesture, and then they both turned to watch the SWAT team approach the grocery store. The men in black moved with military precision, jogging down the dirt road, sticking close to the buildings. If the *Chead* came out of its trance, no one wanted to be caught in the open. While the creatures looked human, they possessed a terrifying speed, and had the strength to tear full-grown men limb from limb.

As the scene inside the grocery store demonstrated.

Absently, Chris clutched his mother's arm tighter. The *Chead* were almost legend throughout the Western Allied States, a dark shadow left over from the days of the American War. The first whispers of the creatures were believed to have started in 2030, not long after the United States had fallen.

At first they had been dismissed as rumour by a country eager to move on from the decade-long conflict of the American War. The attacks had been blamed on resistance fighters in rural communities, who had never fully supported their severance from the United States. So the government had imposed curfews over rural communities and sent in the military to quell the problem.

Meanwhile, the rest of the young nation had moved forward, and prospered. The pacific coast had boomed as migrants arrived from the allied nations of Mexico and Canada, replacing the thousands of lives lost in the American War.

But through the years, reports of attacks continued, and accounts by survivors eventually filtered through to the media. Each claimed the slaughter had been carried out by one or two individuals – often someone well known in the community. One day, they would be an ordinary neighbour, mother, father, child. The next, they would become the monster now standing in the grocery store.

It was not until one of the creatures was captured,

that the government had admitted its mistake. By then, rural communities had suffered almost a decade of terror at the hands of the monstrosities. Newsrooms and government agencies had been beside themselves with the discovery, with blame pointed in every direction from poor rural police-reporting, to secret operations by the Texans to destabilise the Western Allied States.

The government had extended curfews across the entire country and increased military patrols, but the measures had done little to slow the spread of attacks. Last year, in 2050, the first *Chead* sighting had been reported in Los Angeles, and was quickly followed by attacks in Portland and Seattle. Fortunately, they had yet to reach the streets of San Francisco. Even so, a perpetual State of Emergency had been put into effect.

On the television, the SWAT team had reached the grocery store and were now gathering outside, their rifles trained on the entrance. One lowered his rifle and stepped towards it, the others covering him from behind. Reaching the door, he stretched out an arm and began to pull it open.

The *Chead* did not make a sound as it tore through fthe store windows and barrelled into the man. A screech came through the old television speakers as the men scattered before the *Chead's* ferocity. With one hand, it grabbed its victim by the throat and hurled him across the street. The thud as he struck the ground was audible over the reporter's microphone.

The crunch of their companion's untimely demise seemed to snap the other members of the squadron into action. The first bangs of gunfire echoed over the television speakers, but the *Chead* was already moving. It tore across the dirt road as bullets raised dust-clouds around it, and smashed into another squad member. A scream echoed up from the street as man and *Chead* went down, disappearing into a cloud of dust.

Despite the risk of hitting their comrade, the rest of the SWAT team did not stop firing. The chance of survival once a *Chead* had its hands on you was zero to none, and no one wanted to take the chance it might escape.

With a roar, the *Chead* reared up from the dust, then spun as a bullet struck it in the shoulder. Blood blossomed from the wound as it staggered backwards, its grey eyes wide, flickering with surprise. It reached up and touched a finger to the hole left by the bullet, its brow creasing with confusion.

Then the rest of the men opened fire, and the battle was over.

CHAPTER 2

THE SCREEN of the old CRT television flickered to black as Chris's mother moved across and switched it off. Her face was pale when she turned towards him, and a shiver ran through her as she closed her eyes.

"Your Grandfather would be ashamed, Chris," she said, shaking her head. "He went to war against the United States because he believed in our freedom. He fought to keep us free, not to spend decades haunted by the ghosts of the past."

Chris shivered. He'd never met his grandfather, but his mother and grandmother talked of him enough that Chris felt he knew him. When the United States had refused to accept the independence of the Western Allied States, his grandfather had accepted the call to defend their young nation. He had enlisted in the WAS Marines and had shipped off to war. The conflict had quickly expanded to engulf the whole of North America. Only the aid of Canada and Mexico had given the WAS the strength to survive, and eventually prevail against the aggression of the United States.

Unfortunately, his grandfather had not survived to see the world change. He had learned of Chris's birth while stationed in New Mexico, but had never returned to see his grandson grow. So Chris knew him only from photos, and the stories of his mother and grandmother.

"Things will change soon." Chris shook his head. "Surely?"

His mother crinkled her nose. "I've been saying that for ten years," she said as she moved towards the kitchen, ruffling Chris's hair as she passed him, "but things only ever seem to get worse."

Chris moved after her and pulled out a chair at the wooden table. The kitchen was small, barely big enough for the two of them, but it was all they needed. His mother was already standing at the stove, stirring a pot of stew he recognised as leftovers from the beef shanks of the night before.

"Most don't seem to care, as long as the attacks are confined to the countryside," Chris commented.

"Exactly." His mother turned, emphatically waving the wooden spoon. "They think it doesn't matter, that our wealth will protect us. Well, it won't stay that way forever."

"No." Chris shook his head. "That one in Seattle…" he shuddered. Over fifty people had been killed by a single *Chead* in a shopping mall. Police had arrived within ten minutes, but that was all the time it had needed.

Impulsively, he reached up and felt the pocket watch he wore around his neck. His mother had given it to him ten years ago, at his father's funeral. It held a picture of his parents, smiling on the shore of Lake Washington in Seattle, where they had met. His heart gave a painful throb as he thought of the terror engulfing the city.

Noticing the gesture, his mother abandoned the pot and pulled him into a hug. "It's okay, Chris. We'll survive this. We're a strong people. They'll come up with a solution, even if we have to march up to parliament's gates and demand it."

Chris nodded and was about to speak when a crash came from somewhere in the house. They pushed apart and spun towards the kitchen doorway. Though they lived in the city, when Chris's father had passed away they had been forced to move closer to the city's edge. It was not the safest neighbourhood, and it was well past the seven o'clock curfew now. Whoever, or whatever, had made the noise was not likely to be friendly.

Sucking in a breath, Chris moved into the doorway and risked a glance into the lounge. The single incandescent bulb cast shadows across the room, leaving dark patches behind the couch and television. He stared hard into the darkness, searching for signs of movement, and then retreated to the kitchen.

Silently, his mother handed him a kitchen knife. He took it after only a second's hesitation. She held a second blade in a practiced grip. Looking at her face, Chris swallowed hard. Her eyes were hard, her brow creased in a scowl, but he did not miss the fear there. Together they faced the door, and waited.

The squeak of the loose floorboard in the hall sounded as loud as a gunshot in the silent house. Chris glanced at his mother, and she nodded back. There was no doubt now.

A crash came from the lounge, then the thud of heavy boots as the intruder gave up all pretence of stealth. Chris tensed, his knuckles turning white as he gripped the knife handle. He spread his feet into a forward stance, readying himself.

The crack of breaking glass came from their right as the kitchen window exploded inwards, and a black-suited figure tumbled into the room. The man bowled into his mother, sending her tumbling to the ground before she could swing the knife. Chris sprang to the side as another man charged through the doorway to the lounge, then drew back and hurled the knife.

Without pausing to see whether the knife struck home, Chris twisted and leapt, driving his shoulder into the midriff of the intruder standing over his mother. But the man was ready for him, and with his greater bulk brushed Chris off with little effort. Stumbling sideways, Chris clenched his fists and charged again.

The man grinned, raising his arms to catch him. With his attention diverted, Chris's mother rose up behind him, knife still in hand, and drove the blade deep into the attacker's hamstring.

Their black-garbed attacker barely had time to scream before Chris's fist slammed into his windpipe

His face paled and his hands went to his neck. He staggered backwards, strangled noises gurgling from his throat, and toppled over the kitchen table.

Chris offered his mother a hand, but before she could take it a creak came from the floorboards behind him. The man from the lounge loomed up, grabbing Chris by the shoulder before he could leap to safety. Still on the ground, his mother rolled away as Chris twisted around, fighting to break the man's hold. Cursing, he aimed an elbow at the man's gut, but his arm struck solid body armour and bounced off.

That explains the knife, the thought raced through his mind, before another crash from the window chased it away.

Beside him, his mother surged to her feet as a third man came through the window. Still holding the bloodied knife, she screamed and charged the man. Straining his arms, Chris bucked against his captor's grip, but there was no breaking the man's iron hold. Stomach clenched, he watched his mother attack the heavily-armed assailant.

The fresh intruder carried a long steel baton in one hand, and as she swung her knife it flashed out and caught her wrist. His mother screamed and dropped the knife, then retreated across the room cradling her arm. A fourth man appeared through the door to the lounge. Before Chris could shout a warning, he grabbed her from behind.

His mother shrieked and threw back her head, trying to catch the man in the chin, but her blows bounced off his body armour. Her eyes widened as his arm went around her neck, cutting off her breath. Heart hammering in his chest, Chris twisted and kicked at his opponent's shins, desperate to aid his mother, but the man showed no sign of relenting.

"*Mum!*" He screamed as her eyes drooped closed.

"Fallow, situation under control. You're up." The man from the window spoke into his cuff. He moved across to his fallen comrade, whose face was turning purple. "Hold on, soldier. Medical's on its way."

"Who are you?" Chris gasped.

The man ignored him. Instead, he went to work on the fallen man. Removing his belt, he bound it around the man's leg. The injured man groaned as the speaker worked, his eyes closed and his teeth clenched. A pang of guilt touched Chris, but he crushed it down.

"What the hell happened?" Chris looked up as a woman appeared in the doorway.

The woman was dark-skinned, but the colour rapidly fled her face as her gaze swept over the kitchen. She raised a hand to her mouth, her eyes lingering on the blood, then flicking between the men and their captives. Shock showed in their amber depths, but already it was fading as she reasserted control. Lowering her hand to her side, she pursed her red lips. Her gaze settled on Chris.

A chill went through Chris as he noticed the red emblazoned bear on the front of her black jacket. The symbol marked her as a government employee.

These were not random thugs in the night – they were police, and they were here for Chris and his mother.

Taking a breath, the woman nodded to herself, then reached inside her jacket and drew something into the light. The breath went from Chris's chest as he glimpsed the steel contraption in her hand. For a second he thought it was a pistol, but as she drew closer he realised his mistake. It was some sort of hypodermic gun, some medical contraption he had seen in movies, though in real life it looked far more threatening, more deadly.

"Who are you?" Chris croaked as she paused in front of him.

Her eyes drifted to Chris's face, but she only shook her head and looked away. She studied the liquid in the vial attached to the gun's barrel, then at Chris, as though weighing him up.

"Hold him," she said at last.

"What?" Chris gasped as his captor's hands pulled his arms behind his back. "What are you doing? Please, you're making some mistake, we haven't done anything wrong!"

The woman did not answer as she raised the gun to his neck. Chris struggled to move, but the man only pulled his arms harder, sending a bolt of pain through his shoulders. Biting back a scream, Chris looked up at the woman. Their eyes met, and he thought he saw a flicker of regret in the woman's eyes.

Then the cold steel of the hypodermic gun touched his neck, followed by a hiss of gas as she pressed the trigger. Metal pinched at Chris's neck for a second, before the woman stepped back. Holding his breath, Chris stared at the woman, his eyes never leaving hers.

Within seconds the first touch of weariness began to seep through Chris's body. He blinked as shadows spread around the edges of his vision. Idly, he struggled to free his arms, so he might chase the shadows away. But the man still held him fast. Sucking in a mouthful of air, Chris fought against the exhaustion. Blinking hard, he stared at the woman, willing himself to resist the pull of sleep.

But there was no stopping the warmth spreading through his limbs. His head bobbed and his arms went limp, until the only thing keeping him upright was the strength of his captor.

The woman's face was the last thing Chris saw as he slipped into the darkness.

CHAPTER 3

LIZ SHIVERED as the air conditioner whirred, sending a blast of icy air in her direction. Wrapping her arms around herself, she closed her eyes and waited for it to pass. The scent of chlorine drifted on the air, its chemical reek setting her head to pounding. Her teeth chattered and she shuddered as the whir of fans died away. Groaning, Liz opened her eyes and returned to studying her surroundings.

Ten minutes ago, she had woke in this thirty-foot room, enclosed by the plain, unadorned concrete walls and floor. A door stood on the opposite wall, a small glass panel revealing a bright hallway beyond. It offered the only escape from the little room, but it might as well have been half a world away. Between Liz and the door stood the wire mesh of her little steel cage.

Shaking, she gripped the wire tight in her fingers and placed her head against it. Silently, she searched the vaults of her memories, struggling to find a cause for her current predicament. But she had no memory of how she had come to be there, lying shivering on the concrete floor of a cage.

She cursed as the blast of the air conditioner returned. Her thin clothes were little better than rags, fine in the warm Californian climate, but completely inadequate for the freezing temperatures the central heating system had apparently been set too. To make matters worse, her boots were gone, along with the blade she kept tucked inside them. Without it she felt naked, exposed inside the tiny cage.

At least I'm not alone, she thought wryly, looking through the wire into the cage beside her.

A young man somewhere around her own eighteen years lay there, still dozing on the concrete floor. His clothes were better kept than her own, though there was a bloodstain on one sleeve. From the quality of the shirt he wore, she guessed he was from the city. His short-cropped brown hair and white skin only served to confirm her suspicions.

With a low groan, the boy began to stir. Idly, she wondered what he would make of the nightmare he was about to awake too.

Liz shivered, not from the cold now, but dread. She cast her eyes around the room one last time, desperate for something, *anything*, that might offer escape. As a child, her parents had often warned her of what happened to those who drew the government's ire. Though they were never reported, disappearances had been common in her village. Adults, children, even entire families were known to simply disappear overnight. Though few were brave enough to voice their suspicions out loud, everyone knew who had taken them.

It seemed that after two years on the run, those same people had finally caught up with Liz.

The clang of the door as it opened tore Liz from her musings. Looking up, she saw two men push their way past the heavy steel door. They wore matching uniforms of black pants and green shirts, along with the gold-and-red embossed badges of bears that marked them as soldiers. Both carried a rifle slung over one shoulder, and moved with the casual ease of professional killers.

Liz straightened as the men's eyes drifted over to her cage, refusing to show her fear. Even so, she had to suppress a shudder as wide grins split their faces. Scowling, she crossed her arms and stared them down.

"Feisty one, ain't she?" the first said in a strong Californian accent. Shaking his head, he moved past the cages to a panel in the wall.

"Looks like the boy's still asleep," the other commented as he joined the first. "Gonna be a nasty wake-up call."

Together, they pulled open the panel and retrieved a hose. Thick nylon strings encased the outer layer of the hose, and a large steel nozzle was fitted to its end. Dragging it across the room, they pointed it at the sleeping boy and flipped a lever on the nozzle.

Water gushed from the hose and through the wire of the cage to engulf the unconscious young man. A blood-curdling scream echoed off the walls as he seemed to levitate off the floor, and began to thrash against the torrent of water.

Liz bit back laughter as another scream came, half gurgled by the water. The men with the hose showed no such restraint, and their laughter rang through the room. They ignored the young man's strangled cries, holding the water steady until it seemed he could not help but drown in the torrent.

When they finally shut off the water, the boy collapsed to the floor of his cage, gasping for breath. He shuddered, spitting up water, but the men were already moving towards Liz, and she had no more time to consider his predicament.

She raised her hands as the men stopped in front of her cage. "No need for that, boys. I'm already clean, see?" She did a little turn, her cheeks warming as she sensed their eyes on her again.

The men chuckled, but shook their heads. "Sorry girl, boss's orders."

They pulled the lever before Liz could offer any further argument.

Liz gave a strangled shriek as the ice-cold water drove her back against the wire of the cage. She lifted her hands in front of her face, fighting to hold back the water, but it made little difference against the rush. Gasping, she choked as water flooded her throat, and sank to her knees. An icy hand gripped her chest as she inhaled again, turning her back to protect her face. The power of the water forced her up against the wire, and she gripped it hard with her fingers, struggling to hold herself upright.

When the torrent finally ceased, Liz found herself crouched on the ground with her back to the men. She did not turn as a coughing fit shook her body. An awful cold seeped through her bones as she struggled for breath. Water filled her ears and nose, muffling the words of the men until she shook her head to clear it.

Tightened her hold on the wire, Liz used it to pull herself to her feet. Head down, she gave a final cough and faced the room.

The men were already returning the hose to its panel in the wall. They spoke quietly to themselves, but fell silent as the hinges of the door squeaked again. Liz looked up as a group of men and woman entered the room. There were five in total, three men and two women, and each wore a white lab coat with black pants. Four of them carried electronic tablets, their heads bent over the little screens, while the fifth approached the guards. They straightened as he drew up in front of them, their grins fading.

"Are our latest subjects ready for processing?" the man asked, his voice cool.

One of the guards nodded. "Yes, Doctor Halt. We've just finished hosing them down."

A smile twitched at Halt's lips. "Very good," he dismissed the men with a flick of his hand and turned to face the cages.

Pursing his thin lips, Halt moved closer, pacing

around Liz's cage in a slow circle. His eyes did not leave her as he moved, and eventually she was forced to look away. He moved like a predator, his grey eyes studying her like prey, eyeing up which piece of flesh to taste first. Wrapping her arms around herself, Liz fixed her eyes to the concrete and tried to ignore him.

When Liz looked up again, Halt had moved on to studying the young man in the other cage. But her fellow captive was ignoring him. Instead, he stared at the group of doctors, his brow creased with confusion, as though struggling to recall a distant memory.

"*You!*" the boy shouted suddenly, slamming his hands against the wire. "You were at my house! What am I doing here? *What have you done with my mother?*" His last words came out as a shriek.

Halt glanced back at the group of doctors. "Doctor Fallow, would you care to explain why the subject knows your face?"

The woman at the head of the group turned beet red. Biting her lip, she replied. "There were complications during his extraction, Halt," her voice came out soft, but Liz sensed her defiance behind them. "I had to enter before the subject was unconscious, or we risked casualties amongst the extraction team."

Halt eyed her for a moment, apparently weighing up her words before he nodded. "Very well." He turned back to the cages. "No matter. Elizabeth Flores, Christopher Sanders, welcome to the Praegressus Facility."

Cold fingers gripped Liz by the throat, silencing

her voice. They knew her last name. That meant they knew who she was, where she came from. The last trickle of hope slipped from her heart. It was no mistake she had found herself here.

Christopher was not so easily quelled. "What am I doing here? You can't hold us like his, I know my rights—"

Halt raised a hand and her neighbour fell silent. Moving across, Halt stood outside Christopher's cage and stared through the wire. "Your mother has been charged with treason."

Colour fled the boy's face, turning his white skin a sickly yellow. He swallowed and opened his mouth, but no words came out. Tears crystallised at the corner of his eyes, but he blinked them back before they could fall.

Biting her tongue, Liz watched the two stare at one another. She was impressed by Christopher's resilience. He might speak with an urban accent, but it seemed he possessed more courage than half the boys she'd once known in her boarding school. If his mother had been convicted of treason, it meant death for her and her immediate family. A pass was given for the elderly, but there was no such exception for children…

Swallowing, Liz eyed the group still lingering behind Halt. If that was the reason Christopher was here, she didn't like her chances. She had always guessed the authorities might come after her and had done her best to avoid detection. With cameras on every street corner, she had been forced to keep to the countryside she knew so well. Even then, she had always known it would only be a matter of time before someone found her.

Even so, she wanted to find out how much they really knew about her.

CHAPTER 4

"WHAT ABOUT ME?" Liz croaked. "My parents are gone. I've done nothing wrong."

Halt's eyes turned towards her and his scowl deepened. "Elizabeth Flores." He paused, looking her up and down with a sneer. "Vagrant, beggar, fugitive. You have escaped justice for long enough. After what your parents did, did you really think we would not come for you? That we would not hunt you to the ends of the earth?"

White-hot fire lit Liz's chest, but she forced herself to take a deep breath and swallow the screams building in her throat. She wanted to deny the accusations, to curse him and the others, but she knew there was no point. She had tried that once before, when they had first come for her. But one look at her ragged clothes, at the curly black hair and olive skin, and they had dismissed her words as lies.

Her shoulders slumped as Halt looked away. Wrapping her arms around herself, she staggered to the back of the cage and sank to the floor. She wasn't giving up, not yet, but she knew when silence offered the better course of action.

Unlike her fellow prisoner.

"What is this place?" Christopher's voice was soft, as though if he whispered, the answer might offer some sort of mercy.

Liz glanced across at him, and watched as he lost his battle with the tears. Despite herself, a pang of sympathy twitched in her chest. She knew what it was like, to lose her parents. She would not wish it on anyone.

"This is your redemption." Halt spread his arms, including them both in the gesture. "This is your chance to redress the crimes of your parents, to contribute to the betterment of our nation. The government has seen fit to offer you both a reprieve."

"How generous of them," Liz muttered from the floor.

She shivered as Halt's eyes found hers. They flashed with anger, offering a silent warning against further interruptions. Pursing her lips, she gripped the wire tighter. It cut into her fingers as she willed herself to contain her anger.

"My mother was not a traitor," came Christopher's response. "How dare you–"

Halt waved a hand and the guards who still waited at the rear of the room came to life. They marched past the silent group of doctors and approached Chris's cage. One produced a key and a second later they had the door open. Moving inside, there was a brief scuffle as they tried to get their hands on the boy. One staggered back from a blow to the face, before the other managed to use his bulk to pin Christopher to the wire.

When they both had a firm grip on him, they hauled him out and forced him to his knees in front of Halt. The doctor loomed over the boy, his arms folded. He contemplated Chris with eyes empty of compassion, like a spider studying a fly trapped in its web. Liz watched on in silence, hardly daring to breathe as Halt nodded to the guards.

The one on the left drew back his boot and slammed it into Christopher's stomach. He collapsed without a sound, his mouth wide, gasping like a fish out of water. A low wheeze came from his throat as he rolled onto his back and strained for breath. It came in a sudden rush, before the boot crashed into his side, almost lifting him off the ground.

A scream tore from the young man's throat as he rolled into a ball. But the other guard only grabbed him by the back of the shirt and hauled him back to his knees. The two of them looked back at Halt then, waiting for further instruction.

Smiling, Halt approached, one finger tapping idly against his elbow. Softly, he continued as though nothing had changed. "As I was saying, you have been given a reprieve, but the crimes of your parents still stand, as does the sentence on your lives. That makes you dead in the eyes of the state. You are no one, nothing but what we permit you to be. If you're lucky, you might find yourselves worthy of our work here at the Praegressus Facility." Liz shivered at the name. It sounded Latin, though she had no idea what it might mean. "More likely though, you will die. But know at least your deaths will have advanced the interests of our fine nation."

Chris still knelt on the ground between the guards, his breath coming in ragged gasps. Halt eyed him, as though weighing whether his words had sunk in, before continuing.

"In the meantime, you will come to respect and obey your betters," Halt spoke. "Soon, you will be shown to your new accommodation. But first, I want to be sure you understand the gravity of your situations. Christopher Sanders, why are you here?"

On the ground, Chris looked up at the doctor. His eyes shone, but no tears fell. Turning his head to the side, he spat on the concrete and scowled. "She's a terrible cook," he coughed, then continued, "but I'd hardly say that makes her a traitor–"

The guard's fist caught him on the side of the head and sent him crashing to the floor. A boot followed, and for the next thirty seconds the room rang with the thud of hard leather boots on flesh, interspersed with Christopher's muffled cries. When the guards finally pulled back, the young man lay still, a low groan the only sign of life.

"Get him up," Halt commanded.

Together the guards hauled the boy back to his knees. This time Halt leaned down, until the two of them were face to face. "Well?"

Christopher's shoulders sagged and his head

bowed. A soft sob came from his mouth, and for a second she thought he would not speak. Then he nodded, and a whisper followed. "Okay," he croaked, "okay... My mother... was a traitor." He looked up as he finished, a spark of flame still burning in his eyes. "*Does that make you happy?*"

The doctor eyed him for a long while, as though measuring up his admission with the show of defiance. Finally he nodded, and the guards grabbed Christopher by the shoulders and muscled him back into the cage.

The clang as the door closed sent a thrill of ice down Liz's spine. She stared down at the floor, sensing the eyes of the room on her, and waited for Halt to address her.

"Ah, Elizabeth Flores," his voice snaked its way around her, raising the hackles on her neck. "You have run for so long. Surely you at least must admit to your parents' crimes?"

Looking up, Liz found the cold grey eyes of the doctor watching her. She suppressed a shudder and quickly looked away. Taking slow, measured breaths, she beat down the rage burning in her chest. She took one step, then another, until she reached the front of her cage. Leaning against the wire, she looked down at the doctor and raised an eyebrow.

"What would you like me to admit too?" she whispered.

Halt took a step back from the cage, but she did not miss the way his eyes lingered on her. She gave a little smirk as he growled. "Disgusting girl," he spat.

"Admit that your parents were monsters - that you aided them, that for years you have run from the law, hiding from justice."

A tremble of rage raced through Liz. She bit her lip. Closing her eyes, she sent out a silent prayer for the souls of her parents. Their faces drifted through her mind – smiling, happy, at peace. They had been kind and sweet, only ever wanting for her to be happy, to have a better life than the one they'd lived. For years they had scraped and saved their every penny, so they could send her to boarding school. The day she'd been accepted, she had never seen them so happy. And for three years, she had suffered the taunts of her peers in that school to keep them that way.

But they were long gone now; they did not care what was said about them. There was no need for Liz to suffer now, to bleed for their memory. Not now, when there was no hope of escape. But silently she made a vow to herself, to bide her time and conserve her strength, until an opportunity showed itself.

When she opened her eyes again, she found the cold grey eyes of Halt looking back, and smirked.

"Fine, I admit it. My parents were monsters. What of it?"

She almost laughed as the doctor's face darkened, an angry red flushing across his cheeks. He clenched his fists and made to approach the cage before stopping himself. Flashing a glance over his shoulder at their audience, he shook his head and smiled.

"Very good," he eyed the two of them. "So, we understand one another."

CHAPTER 5

CHRIS GRIPPED the wire of his cage as Halt eyed the two of them. Clamping his mouth shut, he ignored the voice in his head that screamed for answers. His jaw and back ached where the guards had struck him, and he was not eager to repeat the experience. The ugly thugs were grinning at him now, as though daring him to give them another chance. Instead, he bit his tongue and waited to see what came next.

His mind was still reeling, struggling to put together the pieces of his scattered memories. Images from the night flashed through his mind – the *Chead* on the television, the men in his house, his mother falling.

Ice wrapped around his throat as Halt's words twisted in his mind.

Traitor.

A tremor ran through him and he suppressed a sob. The sentence for treason was death. Often just the accusation of such a crime was enough. And now his mother had been taken, stolen away by the woman in the white coat.

Holding his breath, Chris struggled with his fear, his terror that she might already be gone. That he might now be alone, an orphan in a harsh, unforgiving world.

With a low moan, Chris took a great, shuddering breath and shook his head. That was the least of his problems. Whatever his mother's fate, he could do nothing for her now, trapped in this cage.

Opening his eyes, he looked across as Halt spoke. "Now that we have an understanding, we must prepare you for the project." A thin smile spread across his lips. "Take off your clothes."

A chill spread through Chris's chest as Halt folded his arms. Behind him, the guards shifted, edging close, wide grins splitting their faces. A sharp intake of breath came from the other cage, but otherwise the girl did not move.

Chris shrank back from the wire. "Why?"

Halt took a step forward. "Now, Christopher, I had hoped we had moved past this. The dog does not question his master when he is told to sit."

Clenching his fists, Chris shook his head. His eyes travelled past Halt, to the audience of doctors. They lingered on the face of the woman, the doctor called Fallow. "This isn't right," he breathed.

Letting out a long sigh, Halt waved the guards forward. They approached the cage, shoulders hunched, moving with a cold proficiency. Chris hesitated as they reached the door and fumbled with the latch. Then he began to unbutton his shirt, his cheeks flushing with embarrassment.

Outside the guards paused, looking back at Halt in question. The doctor nodded curtly, and they retreated to their positions behind him.

In the cage, Chris quickly stripped off his clothing piece by piece, shivering as the icy breath of the air conditioner brushed across his skin. The hairs stood up on the back of his neck as he pulled off his last strip of clothing and tossed it to the floor. Turning sideways, he bowed his head, struggling to cover himself.

Then, reaching up he unclipped the chain that still hung around his neck. It came away easily, the little pocket watch falling into his hand. He clenched it in his fist, a tremble of grief washing through him. Flicking open the metal catch, he looked at the faces of his mother and father, at their kind smiles, and then closed it again.

Struggling to hold back his tears, he placed the pocket watch gently, reverently on his pile of clothes.

Standing, he felt the eyes of the doctors roaming over his naked flesh, examining him, seeking out his every secret. A deep sense of helplessness rose in his chest, threatening to overwhelm him. Cheeks flushed, he stared hard at the ground, fighting to ignore the world.

"Very good, Christopher," Halt's voice was patronising, and Chris almost choked on the shame that rose in his throat, "and you, Elizabeth?"

Out of the corner of his eye, Chris caught movement from the other cage. Turning his head, he watched as Elizabeth approach the front of the cage. Her lips were pulled into a smirk, but her blue eyes flashed with a barely concealed anger. She pressed herself against the wire and stared across at Halt.

"Come and get me," she growled, her voice threatening.

Chris's eyes widened. After her earlier acquiescence, he had not expected her to resist.

In front of the cages, Halt gave a slow shake of his head. "Bring her," he hissed.

The guards marched passed him and yanked the door to the cage open. Elizabeth retreated from the door, watching as the first of the men pushed their way inside. Then, with a wild shriek, she leapt. At maybe one hundred and twenty-five pounds, she was dwarfed by the guard. Even so, her sudden attack caught him by surprise and sent him tumbling backwards into his comrade.

As the two of them went down in a heap, Elizabeth leapt for the door. She made it over the threshold before the first guard managed to stagger upright. His arm swung out, catching her by the leg, and she slammed into the concrete outside the cage. With another screech, she kicked out with her free leg, catching the guard in the face. He gave a muffled curse, but held on.

In seconds the other guard was up. He strode across to where Elizabeth fought to free herself, reached down, and wrapped one meaty hand around her hair. The girl gave a pained cry as he lifted her up and held her off the ground. She kicked feebly at empty air, her hands batting at his chest. Her mouth gaped as the colour fled her face.

With a contemptuous flick of his arm, the guard tossed her aside. Elizabeth crashed hard into the concrete. She struggled to regain her composure, but a heavy boot drove down onto her back, sending her face first into the floor.

Halt walked across and knelt beside the girl, a cold smile on his snakelike lips.

"Elizabeth," Halt's voice was laced now with honey, "be a good girl now. You cannot join the project with those reminders of your old life. Remove your clothes."

Chris shuddered as the man stood, his grey eyes flashing as he watched the girl lift herself to her hands and knees. One trembling hand reached for the buttons of her shirt and began to pluck them open. Closing his eyes, Chris looked away, unwilling to participate in her shaming.

He glanced back up a few minutes later as the sound of metal striking concrete rang through the room. His eyes were drawn to the object now lying on the ground between Halt and the shivering girl. The thick steel links of a chain lay between them like a snake, the silver metal shining in the fluorescent lights. For an instant, he wondered where it had come from, but his thoughts quickly turned to what it was.

A collar.

CHAPTER 6

"Put it on," Halt's voice slivered through the room, cold, commanding.

Elizabeth flinched away from him, but the guard's hand flashed out and caught her by the hair. Dragging her forward, he shoved her back to her knees in front of the collar. A tremble went through the girl as she glared up at Halt, her eyes flashing. For a second, Chris thought she would resist, but then with a trembling hand she reached out and picked up the collar.

Elizabeth's mouth twisted with disgust as she held the steel linked chain in front of her. Her eyes closed, her nostrils flaring as she sucked in a breath. Chris waited, his own breath held, aware his turn would come soon.

"This is what you want, you disgusting—" the girl broke off as the guard's fist sent her reeling.

A low groan came from her lips, but she straightened on the ground, the collar still in hand. She looked at Halt, and then away again. With trembling hands, she lifted the collar to her throat. The *click* it made as it fastened echoed loudly in the concrete room.

Halt smiled and clapped his hands. The guards grabbed Elizabeth by each arm and hauled her back up. With a few shoves they had her back in the cage, and the steel door swung shut behind her. Then Halt's grey eyes turned towards Chris, where he still waited naked inside his own cage.

"I suppose it's my turn then?" He asked with false bravado.

Halt stared him down, the grey eyes piercing him through. Horror curled its way up Chris's throat as he felt his cheeks warming. His eyes drifted towards the other doctors, who still stood in silence. Outside, the guards approached his cage. Watching them, he saw that one carried a bundle of orange clothing, the other a steel link collar identical to the one Elizabeth now wore.

"Move to the back of the cage," one guard ordered.

Clenching his fists, Chris stumbled back from the door as the guard flicked the latch and pushed it open. His body ached from his beating, and in the narrow space he didn't like his chances of besting the two men. He had already watched the girl take that approach and fail. He would have to wait, bide his time until an opportunity arose.

Inside the cage, the first of the guards collected his clothes and replaced them with the orange bundle. The collar was placed on top of the pile, and then the two men retreated, swinging the door shut behind them.

Chris looked across at Halt, waiting for an order. When none was forthcoming, he moved across to the pile and picked up the collar. Raising an eyebrow, he tried and failed to suppress his sarcasm. "What are we? Your pets now?"

Halt smirked. "Would you like another lesson, Christopher?"

Letting out a long breath, Chris shook his head. He squeezed his fingers, letting the cold metal of the collar dig into his flesh. His heart pounded hard in his chest, screaming a warning, that if he obeyed now there would be no going back.

Dimly, he remembered a story his father had told him when he was younger. It had been almost ten years since the cancer had taken him, but he could still recall his father's voice with crystal clarity. His rough baritone drifted up from Chris's memories, as he described how the *Mahouts* in Thailand had once tamed their elephants.

The *Mahouts* had placed chains around the legs of young elephants and attached them to heavy pegs in the ground. Whenever the elephants tried to escape, the chain would contract, cutting into the elephant's leg, making it bleed. Eventually the elephant would realise the futility of trying to escape.

As adults, the same chain and peg were used to restrain the giant creatures. And though they then possessed the strength to escape the peg and chain, they never tried.

There had been a point to his father's tale, but for the life of him, Chris could not recall its meaning now. Instead, he stared down at the collar, wondering if he was about to take the first step into his own captivity.

But he had no choice but to obey.

With deliberate slowness, Chris raised the collar to his neck. A tingle ran through his skin as the metal touched the flesh of his throat, and a terrifying dread rose within him. A voice screamed for him to run, to hurl the collar away from him.

Instead, he closed his eyes and pulled the collar closed around his neck. The steel links slid across his flesh like the coils of a python, icy to the touch, and came together with a loud click.

Struggling to breathe, Chris sank to his knees and fumbled for the pile of clothes. A sudden, desperate shame at his nakedness took him. He felt exposed, as though his nudity highlighted his new bondage, relegating him to little better than an animal.

Scrambling into the bright orange uniform, he sank back to his knees. A sick despair rose in his throat, but he pushed it down, struggling to keep a flicker of hope above the rising waters. The collar's icy grip tightened around his throat, stealing away his breath. A claustrophobic scream grew in his throat as he coughed for air.

Halt only gave a satisfied nod and stepped back from the cage.

Glancing across at the other cage, he saw Elizabeth had managed to pull on an orange jumpsuit of her own. The heavy fabric clung to her lithe frame, and Chris couldn't help but think of what he had glimpsed of her earlier. A dark bruise showed on her forehead as her clear blue eyes flickered in his direction. His cheeks warmed as she raised an eyebrow and brushed a lock of hair from her face. The wild black curls hung around her shoulders, the ends jagged and split, as though they had been cut by a knife.

Taking a breath, the girl pulled herself to her feet. The collar flashed around her neck, an all too vivid reminder of their captivity. Her fists clenched and her lips drew back in a snarl, but otherwise she remained quiet.

In front of the cages, Halt gave a satisfied smirk. "Very good. I'm pleased to see you are both fast learners. Perhaps you will surprise me." Chris flinched as Halt clapped his hands again. "Now, before you are taken to your new accommodations, I must warn you, I have little patience for agitators. Dissent will not be tolerated. Those collars around your necks are more than they appear. Do not attempt to remove them. Any effort to tamper with them without the correct key will trigger a small explosive discharge, which will have… unpleasant results."

Chris swallowed hard. A trick of sweat ran down his neck and he tasted bile in his throat. Clenching his teeth, he sucked in a breath and fought to keep himself from throwing up whatever remained in his stomach. In the opposite cage, Elizabeth showed no sign she had heard Halt's words. She stood with eyes closed, one arm against the cage wall, as though that was the only thing keeping her upright.

When neither of them spoke, Halt continued. "As we have no wish to risk our guards every time our subjects step out of line, the collars are used as a disciplinary tool."

Leaning against the wall of his cage, Chris stifled a fake yawn, unwilling to show his fear. "Seems a little harsh, blowing off someone's head for a bit of back talk."

The doctor glared at him, then gave a slow shake of his head. "Perhaps you are not as quick to learn as I thought," he raised his arm and pulled down his sleeve.

He wore a sleek black watch around his wrist, all shining metal and glass. As he tapped its surface, the screen glowed bright blue. Another tap and a loud beep came from Chris's collar. The hairs on his neck stood up as Halt looked back at him.

"Your collars are capable of delivering an electric shock of five hundred volts and up to one hundred milliamps. They are activated remotely by these watches, which you will find all personnel within the facility are equipped with." A slow grin spread across Halt's face. "A simple tap of the screen, by any doctor or guard, and all collars within a twenty-foot radius are activated. Or an individual subject's collar may be chosen at our discretion. Perhaps you would like a demonstration?"

Holding his breath, Chris shook his head. From

the corner of his eye, he saw the girl make the same gesture.

Halt eyed the two of them, his eyes lit with a strange light. "You don't seem too enthusiastic," he laughed. "Too bad." Before anyone could move he pressed a thumb to the watch.

Chris opened his mouth to scream as the collar around his neck gave a loud beep. Before a sound could escape him, fingers of fire wrapped around his throat, cutting off his cry. His jaw locked hard as electricity surged through his body. His back arched with sudden agony, and the strength went from his legs, sending him toppling to the concrete. A burning cramp tore through his muscles as he thrashed against the ground. Damp water still pooling on the concrete soaked through his new clothes, but he barely noticed.

A loud buzzing filled his ears, but through it, he could hear Halt's voice. "This is twenty milliamps. Enough to deliver a painful shock, even freeze your motor functions. Not enough to kill – or at least, not over short periods of time."

Another beep sounded and the flow of electricity ceased. Chris slumped to the ground, eyes closed, a low moan crackling up from his chest. The sudden absence of pain was a sweet relief, He sucked in an eager breath, the cold air burning in his throat.

As the last twitch in his muscles faded away, he cracked open his eyes and looked through the wire mesh. He had fallen on his side and now found himself looking through the wire at Elizabeth. She was on the ground as well, her tangled hair covering her face, her limbs splayed out across the concrete. Her forehead sported a nasty cut where she must have struck the ground.

Halt stood between the cages, the same dark grin twisting his face. His eyes found Chris's, and the smile spread.

"Welcome to the Praegressus Project."

CHAPTER 7

Angela Fallow waited until the door closed behind her before allowing her mask to crack. A sharp sob cut the air as she stumbled across the room and collapsed onto the bed. The soft duvet cushioned her fall, but it did nothing for the burden weighing on her soul. Burying her head in a pillow, she finally allowed the tears to flow.

What have I done?

For years she had worked in government laboratories, studying the creatures that had come to be known as the *Chead*, examining their genetic composition and identifying chromosomal alterations within their DNA. While the more superstitious citizens of the Western Allied States regarded the *Chead* as some paranormal phenomenon, she had dedicated her life to dissecting the mysteries of the creatures.

She had been the first to discover the link between the *Chead* awakenings across the country. A short sequence of nucleic acids discovered in one of the samples put her on the trail, and within days she had confirmed her suspicion. Whether the *Chead* had woken in rural Washington or downtown Los Angeles, the same virus was present in the genome of every known *Chead*.

Porcine Endogenous Retrovirus, or PERV, a well-known retrovirus amongst the scientific community. Since the turn of the twentieth century, the virus had been used to exchange DNA between pig and human cells. PERV was a provirus – meaning it fully integrated into the host genome. This led to its use in the modification of genes within the organs of pigs, to increase their receptivity when transplanted into human subjects.

But Angela had checked the records of every *Chead*, and none had ever been a candidate for xenotransplantation.

Normally, the presence of the virus alone would have meant little. There was not a person alive whose chromosome did not contain some viral elements. In fact, many scientists speculated the alterations caused by proviruses played a significant role in evolution, altering genes and alleles at a rate far faster than ordinary mutation.

However, once the link had been discovered, it had not taken Angela long to piece out other discrepancies in the *Chead* chromosomes. Alongside the PERV recombinations, she identified genome markers with foundations in everything from primates to canines, eagles to rabbits. Even genes from rare animals such as the Philippine Tarsier and the

Western Australian Taipan had featured in the genetic puzzle presented by the *Chead*.

In the end, the evidence all pointed to a single, undeniable conclusion.

The *Chead* were no accident. Someone had created them, designed a virus and released it into the world.

The question of who remained unanswered, though the government had quickly pointed the blame on that old enemy – the United States. Or at least the scattered remnant states remaining of the once-great-nation.

But that was not Angela's concern. Now knowing the cause, she had applied herself to countering its spread. Fortunately, the virus did not appear to be contagious. No cases had been reported of friends or family contracting the virus from awakened *Chead*, though the government still rounded them up as a precaution.

That left the question of how the victims were infected. She suspected an outside source was at work there, though again, it was up to others to solve that puzzle.

As for those already infected by the virus, Angela had quickly ruled out a cure. Ordinary viruses incorporated themselves into the host DNA, much as the *Chead* virus had done. However, the similarities ended there. Symptoms of an ordinary viral infection arose when a virus began self-replication, eventually leading to cell rupture and the spread of virons to other cells. Sickness showed as human cells were hijacked by the virons and used for further self-replication.

Instead of following this route, the *Chead* virus remained latent within the cells. It appeared to be almost perfectly incorporated into the human chromosomes of the *Chead* subjects. The alterations exhibited by the *Chead* were the result of gene expression in the cells themselves – the first symptoms only showing once those genes activated. This was similar to how many babies possessed blue eyes for their first few weeks, until genes for brown eyes were activated.

In other words, the virus was a part of the *Chead* now. There was no reversing the process.

Upon learning of Angela's discovery, the government had decided to take her research in a new direction.

Now she was close to an answer – closer than they'd ever been before. Initial trials on bovine subjects had proven successful, but Halt and his government overseers wanted more. They were desperate for an answer, for a beacon of hope to hold up to the people. Even the usually ice cold Halt had appeared flustered in recent weeks, and she sensed far more than her career rested on what happened over the next few weeks and months.

Shivering, Angela wrapped her arms tight around herself. Not for the first time, she wondered what her life would have been like, had she taken a different path. Deep in her soul, she still longed for the wild open space of the countryside, the endless stars and unmarked horizons. Her family's ranch had been remote, far from the bustling hives of the cities – though of course, they did not really own it. They had worked the land, harvested the crops, while the landowner in the city took the profits.

As a young girl, she had resented that fact, and the limitations of rural life. So she had studied and schemed, and won a place in a scholarship programme in Los Angeles. She had grasped the opportunity with both hands, and run off to find her place in the big wide world.

Funny how things changed, with thirty-five years' worth of wisdom.

The world was a wild place too, but in the city, life was far less forgiving than the country.

Angela shuddered as she heard again the awful screams, watched as the girl writhed on the floor of the cage. In the silence of her mind, Angela imagined the girl's blue eyes seeking her out, begging for help.

Another sob tore from Angela's throat. Those eyes, that face; they were so like her own. In those youthful features, she saw her past, saw the girl she had once been reflected back.

What have I done?

The question came again, persistent. She had never thought it would come to this. When Halt had told her their plan to gather candidates for human trials, it had seemed simple. Family members convicted of treason were destined to suffer the same fate as the accused. So why not make use of those lives?

Young, healthy candidates were needed for the

trials to maximise the chances of success. The children of traitors seemed the perfect answer to their needs.

Only now she faced the reality of that decision, it was more awful than she could ever have imagined. Halt might see them as a means to an end, but Angela could not look past the humanity in their eyes. Halt was a monster, seeming to delight in the breaking of each new candidate, but for Angela, the guilt ate at her soul.

On the bed, she heard again the crunch of fists on flesh. Her stomach swirled and it was all she could do not to throw up.

"What have I done?" she whispered.

The plain walls of her private quarters offered no answers, only their silent judgement. This was her life, this little white room, the empty double bed, the white dresser and coat rack beside the door. Her wool fleece hung on the rack, untouched for weeks now.

Staring at it, Angela was taken by an impulse to escape, to leave this place and walk out into the wilderness beyond the facilities walls. Standing, she strode across and tore the coat from the rack. Swinging it around her shoulders, she fastened the buttons and pushed open the door.

The corridor outside ran left and right. Left led deeper into the facility, where her laboratory and the prison rooms waited. She turned right, moving past the closed doors of the other living quarters. It was well past midnight, and the other staff would have retired long ago. Only the night guards would be awake now.

It only took a few minutes to reach the outer door – a fire exit, but from past excursions she knew there was no alarm attached. The heavy steel door watched her approach, unmoved by her sorrow. Placing her shoulder to it, she gave a hard shove and pulled at the latch.

A long screech echoed down the corridor, followed by a blast of cold wind.

Clenching her teeth, Angela pushed it wider and slipped out into the darkness. She pulled the cloak tighter around herself as a tendril of ice slid down her back, and listened as the door clicked shut behind her. She wasn't concerned – there were no locks on the outer doors. Out here, break-ins were the least of their worries.

Angela sucked in a long breath of the mountain air and looked up at the sky. A thousand pinpricks of light dotted the darkness, the full scope of the Milky Way laid bare before her. The pale sliver of a crescent moon cast dim shadows across the rocky ground, where a thin layer of snow dotted the stones. Beyond the light coming from the building behind her, the night beckoned.

Shivering, Angela watched her breath mist in the freezing air. It was eerie, staring out into the absolute black. Other than the sky, not a pinprick of light showed beyond the facility. They were far from civilisation here, miles into the mountains, as remote as one could be within the Western Allied State. Or the WAS, as it had come to be known.

Staring at the stars, Angela could almost imagine herself a child again. A desperate yearning rose within her, to return to the simplicity of life then, to the warmth of her family ranch.

Sucking in another breath, Angela watched the darkness, imagining the long curves of the hidden mountains. The first snow had arrived a few days ago, heralding the onset of winter. Climatologists were predicting a strong *El Nino* though, which would mean a mild winter.

Standing there in the darkness, with the icy wind biting at her skin, Angela could not help but disagree. This winter would be long and savage, and few at the facility would survive its coming. Only the strongest would endure.

She hoped the candidates would prove up to the challenge. They had only one chance, one opportunity. Fail now, and the government would end it all.

Bowing her head, Angela turned back to the fire door. She pushed it open and returned to the warm light of the corridor. Once back inside, she leaned back against the door and slid to the floor.

Just a little longer, she clung to the thought.

Just a little longer, and she could rest, could put this all behind her.

Just a little longer, and she would save the world.

CHAPTER 8

CLANG.

Liz flinched as the cell door swung closed behind her, the harsh sound slashing through her self-control. She clenched her fists, fighting to control the shiver running through her body. Every fibre of her being screamed for her to panic, to run and hide, but she sucked in a breath instead, calming her trembling nerves. Cold steel pressed against her throat, a constant reminder of her captivity.

A sharp pain came from her palms as her nails dug into flesh. With a great effort, she unclenched her fists. The breath caught in her throat, but she swallowed and sucked in another, refusing to give into her panic. The heavy threads of the orange uniform rubbed against her skin, though in truth its quality was better than anything she'd scavenged in the past two years.

Staring ahead, Liz cast her eyes over her new home. The plain concrete walls matched what she'd glimpsed of the rest of the facility on the short trip from cage to prison cell. The journey had taken less than five minutes, a quick march down long corridors, past open doors and strange rooms filled with glass tubes and steel contraptions. Some she recognised from her boarding school: Bunsen burners and beakers, test tubes and cylinders. But the rest was far beyond her understanding – plastic boxes that hummed and whirred, steel cubes of unknown purpose, containers filled with a strange, gel-like substance.

The guards ushered them past each room with quick efficiency, leaving no time for questions. Only once had Liz paused, when they'd passed a room apparently used as a canteen. The smell of coffee and burnt toast wafted out, and she'd seen a dozen people sitting around a table, talking quietly. Before Liz could speak, a guard had jabbed the butt of his rifle into the small of her back.

A little gasp burst from her lips, and several people in had glanced up. Their eyes took her in for a moment, then they looked away, returning to their conversation. Seeing their indifference, Liz had felt the last drops of hope curdle in her chest.

From there they'd been led through a thick iron door, into the grim corridor of a prison block. Faces lined the cells on either side of the corridor as they marched past. Wide eyes stared at them, their owners no more than children, ranging from around thirteen to twenty years of age.

Now Liz stood in a tiny concrete cell, the iron bars

at her back locking her in, sealing her off from the outside world. Two sets of bunk beds had been pushed against the walls on her left and right, while at the rear a toilet and sink were bolted into the floor. Curtains dangled down beside the toilet, presumably to offer some small semblance of privacy.

And between the bunks stood her new roommates.

The boy and girl stared back at Liz and Christopher. The boy stood well over six feet, his muscled shoulders and arms dwarfing the girl beside him. His skin was a dark hue of Native American descent, except where a long white scar stretched down his right arm. Long black hair hung around his razor-sharp face, and hawkish brown eyes studied her with detached curiosity.

Beside him, the girl could not have provided a greater contrast. Her pale white skin shone in the bright overhead lights, unmarked by so much as a freckle, and at around five foot three, she barely came up to the boy's chest. She stood with arms folded, her posture defensive, though with her thin frame Liz guessed she'd struggle to fend off a toddler. Long hair hung down to her waist, the scarlet locks well-trimmed but unwashed. At first glance, Liz thought she might have just walked off a photoshoot.

But with closer reflection, Liz noticed the faint marks of bruises on her arms, the traces of purple on her cheeks and the dark circles beneath her tawny yellow eyes. Cuts and old scars marked her knuckles, and several of her once-long nails were broken.

Maybe not so harmless after all, Liz mused.

The boy from the cages, Christopher, stood beside her, making them a party of four. Although it wasn't much of a party. So far they'd gone a full minute without speaking.

Outside, the last thud of boots ceased and the crash of the outer doors closing heralded the departure of their escort.

Between the bunks, the boy came to life. "Welcome to hell," he spoke in a Washington accent as he offered a hand, "I'm Sam, I'll be your captain today. Ashley here will be your air hostess."

Beside him, Ashley rolled her eyes and pursed her lips, but did not speak.

Liz winced as she recognised the urban twang. She had already dismissed the possibility of the girl being rural, but she had held up hope for the boy at least... A lonely sorrow rose within her as she wrapped her arms around herself. It seemed not only was she to be locked away, but her roommates were going to be a bunch of kids straight out of prep school.

Closing her eyes, she recognised Christopher's voice as he spoke. "Ah..." the boy sounded confused by their new roommate's banter. "My name's Chris, and ah... this is Elizabeth, I guess."

Her ears twitched as she heard the shuffling of feet, no doubt the sound of the two shaking hands. Shivering, she blinked back the sudden tears that sprang to her eyes, determined to keep her weakness to herself. Her head throbbed where the guards had struck her, and a dull ache came from the small of her back.

The tremor came again, the cold air of the room eating at her resistance. Her eyes snapped open, her gaze sweeping her surroundings, finding three sets of eyes studying her closely. A frown creased Sam's forehead and his mouth opened, as though to ask a question, but she looked away before he could speak. A sudden yearning to be alone took her, a need for the peaceful quiet of the country. The concrete walls seemed to be closing on her, the still air suffocating.

Her eyes found the beds, taking in the unmade beds on the bottom. Above them, the sheets of the top bunks were pulled tight, untouched by sleep.

Without a word, she stumbled past Sam and Ashley and grasped at the ladder. Arms shaking, she pulled herself up and rolled onto the hard mattress of her new bed.

"Your girlfriend's a friendly one, Chris," Sam's voice carried up to her, but Liz only closed her eyes, and willed away the sounds. Her breath came in ragged gasps as she tried to still her racing heart.

"She's just scared," was Chris's uncertain reply.

You're wrong, she thought.

She was angry, horrified, frustrated, and more than anything in the world she just wanted to curl up in a corner and cry. But instead, she found herself trapped in a tiny cell with three teenagers from the city – two young men and a girl who would never understand her, her past.

"She should be," Sam's voice took on a bitter tone, "you two haven't even seen the worst of it yet."

Sam's voice put Liz on edge, dragging her back from the peace she sought, but she kept her mouth shut. Scuffling came from below as the three moved, then the bunk shifted beneath her as someone sat on the bed below. Cracking open one eye, Liz saw the two boys still standing, and guessed Ashley had retreated to her bed.

"I don't plan on sticking around to find out," Chris spoke in a hoarse whisper. "I have to get out of here."

Soft laughter followed his statement. "Don't we all, kid," Sam replied jokingly. "But it's kind of a one-way ticket."

"I don't care," Chris's voice smouldered with anger. "Fallow… That woman, she took my mother. I can't, I can't let anything happen to her."

"Tough luck, kid. Wherever she is, she's going to have to cope without you. The only way out of here is in a body bag. Just be glad it wasn't our pal Doctor Halt who grabbed her – although I'm sure he could arrange a reunion if you asked him nicely."

Below, Chris swore. "How can you joke?" he snarled, his voice rising. "Don't you understand? There's been some mistake. My mother hasn't done anything wrong. Her father died in the American War; she would never betray the WAS --"

"And you think our families are any different?" the larger boy snapped back, the humour falling from his voice. "You think we all conspired against the government? Don't be a fool. There's no going back, no changing things now. Not for any of us."

Silence fell over the cell, the only noise the soft breath of those below. A grin tugged at Liz's lips as she embraced the quiet, taking the opportunity to calm her roiling thoughts. The lights were bright overhead, burning through her eyelids, but at least the assault on her ears had ceased. Thinking of the other three, she felt a pang of empathy for them, a sadness for their loss. They were orphans now too, same as her.

Perhaps she was not so alone, after all.

"It doesn't matter," Chris's voice came as a whisper now, "I'll find a way."

Sam chuckled. "You and what army? Even if you could remove that collar, could break out of this cell, where would you go? Who would help you, Chris? You're the son of a traitor, a fugitive without rights."

A rustling came from below, followed by a yelp. Glancing down, her eyes widened as she saw Chris pushing Sam up against the wall.

"She's not a traitor," Chris grated out the words. "And like I said, it doesn't matter. I'm not going to sit here and give up. I'm not going to let them win."

There was no humour in Sam's face now. Scowling, he reached up and with deliberate slowness gripped Chris's hands and removed them from his shirt.

"Listen, *kid*," his voice was threatening now. "You still don't get it, do you? We mean *nothing* to these people. You'll find that out tomorrow, how *little* your life means. They'll kill you the second you cross them."

"Let them try," Chris snapped.

Sam's face darkened, and then it was his turn to grab Chris by the shirt. Without apparent effort, he lifted Chris off the ground, leaving the smaller boy kicking feebly at empty air.

"Believe me, I couldn't care less if you get yourself killed," Sam snapped. "But since we're trapped in here with you, chances are your stupidity will get us *all* executed—"

Sam broke off as Chris twisted in his grasp and drove a foot into the larger boy's stomach. Air exploded between Sam's teeth as he staggered backwards, dropping Chris unceremoniously to the ground. Chris landed lightly on his feet and straightened, eying Sam across the cell.

Liz raised an eyebrow as the two faced each other, their faces twisted with anger.

"*Enough!*" A girl's sharp voice cut the air.

The two boys practically jumped out of their skins as Ashley stood between them. Moving with a cat-like grace, she moved across to Sam and placed a hand on his chest. Her eyes flickered from Sam to Chris, a gentle smile warming her lips.

"Enough," she said again, softly this time. Even so, there was strength in her words.

Liz watched with surprise as Sam's shoulders slumped, the tension fleeing at Ashley's touch. Chris stared, his eyes hesitant, before he lowered his fists. The smile still on her lips, Ashley gave a quick nod.

"We can't fight amongst ourselves," she chided, like a teacher reprimanding her students. "Sam, you know that better than anyone. We need each other."

She turned towards Chris then, her eyes soft. "Chris, I know you're afraid, that you're terrified for your mother. I know it's awful, that you're confused. But you must calm yourself. Your mother would not want you to throw your life away."

Liz blinked, shocked by the calm manner with which Ashley had taken control of the situation. With surprising insight, she had cut straight to the heart of the matter and found a way to quench Chris's rising anger. Despite her reservations, Liz found herself warming to the girl.

Below, Ashley turned back to Sam. "Sam, you can't hide behind that charade. Not from me," she paused, her tawny eyes watching him, "not after everything we've been through."

Sam bowed his head. "You caught me, as usual," he said with a shrug. Pushing past her, he threw himself on his own bed. "I still don't want him getting us all killed though!"

Ashley nodded. Her eyes swept the room, lingering for a second as they caught Liz watching her, before turning to Chris. She moved across to him and placed a hand on his shoulder.

"You are not alone, Chris," she whispered. "Wherever you came from before, we are in this together now. We're family, you and I. All of us," Ashley spoke with words rich in emotion. "And you're right. We can't just give up. We *will* find a way out of here, together. Whoever these people are, they are only human. They're not perfect. Eventually they'll make a mistake, leave some hole in their defences. And when they do, we'll be ready for them, we'll take our chance."

Liz's heart lurched as the yellow eyes flickered back to her. "That goes for you too, Elizabeth."

Warmth spread to Liz's cheeks as the other girl watched her. She nodded slowly, struggling to cover her embarrassment. Listening to Ashley's words, she could almost feel a flicker of hope stir inside her. Maybe the girl was right, maybe she wasn't alone after all. Whatever their differences, Ashley was right. They were in this together now.

Sitting up, Liz placed her hands beneath her and propelled herself off the side of the bed. She landed lightly, her bare feet slapping against the concrete, and straightened in front of Ashley. A smile, genuine now, tugged at her lips, but she tried to maintain a stoic expression. She didn't want to get too far ahead of herself – they were still from the city, after all.

Liz took a deep breath and offered Ashley her hand.

"You can call me Liz."

CHAPTER 9

CHRIS EXHALED hard as he rounded the final bend in the track, his lungs burning with the exertion. Pain tore through his calves and his stomach gave a sickening lurch, but he pressed on. The dirt track gripped easily beneath his bare feet, propelling him on towards the finish line. From behind came the ragged breath of the others, some hot on his tail, others fallen far behind.

Allowing himself a smile, Chris glanced to the side, and almost tripped when he saw Liz draw alongside him. The black-haired girl had her head down, her eyes fixed to the path, and was picking up pace. Panting hard, Chris followed suit, and side by side, the two of them raced down the final straight.

For the last few feet, Chris's feet barely touched the ground. In the corners of his vision, he saw shadows pressing in, exhaustion threatening. Through the darkness, he glimpsed Liz pulling ahead, saw the wild grin spread across her face as she crossed the line a second before him.

Drawing to a stop behind her, Chris shook his head, his mouth unable to form words. Bending in two, he sucked in a mouthful of air. He felt strangely light-headed, his lungs aflame. It took him a full minute to truly catch his breath. By then the others had pulled up nearby.

Lowering himself to the ground, Chris blinked sweat from his eyes. Using one large orange sleeve, he wiped his forehead clear and shook his head at Liz.

"You're fast," he croaked.

It was the second day since their awakening, and since then the two of them had barely spoken. Despite her reluctant greeting in the cell, Liz remained withdrawn. She had been quiet when they spoke in the cell, and said little of her past.

Liz only shrugged. Two blue eyes glanced at him, and then away. "It's the air," she breathed. "We're in the mountains – I can taste it. You're probably not used to the altitude."

Chris nodded, and stars danced across his vision. A groan built in his throat as he saw Liz straighten, but he pushed it down and lifted himself to his feet. Ignoring the ache in his muscles, they moved across to join the others.

Sam and Ashley stood with their hands on their hips, looking like they had barely broken a sweat. Chris cursed himself for exerting so much energy. Who knew what else the day had in store for them.

Yesterday, they had been taken into a laboratory

and put through a series of tests. The doctors had worked with a cool efficiency, asking questions, giving instructions, taking measurements, all the while steadfastly refusing to engage with the captives. Behind the doctors, the guards remained colder still, their hard eyes following the prisoners' every movement.

The tests had been easy, little more than a thorough examination by the local GP. But now it seemed the easy part was over. That morning they had been roused in the early hours by the shriek of a buzzer and the sudden brilliance of the overhead lights. For a few seconds Chris had tried to resist, exhausted after a long night spent tossing and turning, unable to sleep. But Sam and Ashley had been insistent, dragging them from their beds to stand for inspection.

Within minutes, the guards marched past. A doctor accompanied them, pausing outside each cell to make notes on his electronic tablet. Chris shivered as the man's eyes fell on him. There had been a mindless look to him, a mechanical way in which he took the roster, as though this was no more than an inventory check at the grocery store.

When the doctor left, the guards returned with a trolley. The hallway rang with the sound of bowls sliding through metal grates. Chris had stared for a long moment at the oatmeal congealing in his bowl, before the rumbling of his stomach won him over. Resigning himself, he'd taken up his spoon and eaten all he could.

Then their escort of doctors and guards had arrived, taking them from the quiet of their cell and marching them through the facility to this field – if it could be called that. The open space was the size of a football field, but there was not a blade of grass in sight.

Instead, a fine dust covered the ground, spreading out across the oval like snow. A running track ran around its circumference, edged by tall, imposing walls that hemmed them in on all sides. The cold grey concrete stretched up almost thirty feet, interspersed with the metal railings of observation decks. A guard stood at each deck, rifles held in ready arms.

Above the walls, the sun beat down from the cloudless blue sky. The world outside was hidden by the walls, and whether Liz's mountains existed beyond remained a mystery.

Other than the doctors and their escort of guards, the field was empty. The doctors had made quick notes on their ever-present tablets, before nodding to the guards. Orders were barked, and the four of them had set off running.

Now they stood together in a little circle, panting softly as they waited for the next command. The doctors hovered nearby, their eyes fixed on their tablets, talking quietly amongst themselves. The guards still stood beside them, their dark eyes fixed on the prisoners.

Beyond the little group of overseers, a red light started to flash above the door they'd entered through. A buzzer sounded, short and sharp. Beside the doctors, the guards straightened, turning to face the entrance. The door gave a loud click and swung inwards.

Another group of doctors entered, followed by four prisoners in matching orange uniforms. Chris scanned the faces of the doctors, searching for Fallow, but there was no sign of her. His shoulders slumped and he clenched his fists, struggling to contain his disappointment. The woman was his only remaining link to his mother, but she had been conspicuously absent since their initiation.

As the group moved towards them, Chris sensed movement beside him. Glancing at the others, he was surprised to see Sam's face harden, the easy smile slipping from his lips. The older boy reached out and grasped Ashley by the wrist, then nodded in the direction of the newcomers. Ashley's face paled when she saw the group of orange prisoners, and she stumbled sideways a step before Sam caught her.

"What?" Chris hissed.

The two glanced at each other and then shook their heads. "Nothing," Sam muttered.

Before Chris could say anything more, the new group of inmates pulled up across from them. They hovered a few paces away, three boys and a girl, their eyes studying Chris and the others with suspicion. Chris stared back, wondering at the reaction of Sam and Ashley.

Clearing his throat, one of the doctors stepped between the two groups. He glanced at his tablet, then left and right. "Ashley and Samuel. Richard and Jasmine. You have already qualified for the next round of analysis. You are here to ensure your health does not deteriorate."

Chris watched a flicker of discomfort cross the faces of a boy and girl in the opposite group, and guessed they were the ones the man was addressing. Richard sported short blond hair and angry green eyes that did not waver from Ashley and Sam. He was almost a foot shorter than Sam, but more than matched the larger boy for muscle. He kept his arms crossed tight, his stocky shoulders hunched, and a scowl fixed on his face.

The girl, who he guessed was Jasmine, stood head to head beside Richard, a matching glare twisting her red lips. Her hair floated in the breeze, the black locks brushing across her face. The skin around her brown eyes pinched as she turned towards Chris, and caught him staring. Air had hissed between her teeth as she raised one jet-black eyebrow.

Chris quickly looked away, his heart beginning to race. Between them, the doctor had turned his attention on them.

"Elizabeth and Christopher, today we will test your fitness and athleticism, to assess your suitability for the next stage of the program. William and Joshua will be joining you. I suggest you get acquainted."

Chris's eyes drifted over to the other boys, and found them staring back. Their eyes did not hold the same animosity as Jasmine and Richard, just a wary distrust. The one on the left was a scrawny stickman of a figure, his long arms and legs little more than bone. Sharp cheekbones stood out on his face, and his jade-green eyes held more than a hint of fear. The other was larger, his arms well-muscled, but he did not match Richard or Sam for sheer bulk. He stood several inches above Chris's five-foot-eleven, and had long blond hair that hung down around his shoulders.

Seeing neither of the two were about to introduce themselves, Chris made to step towards them. Sam's hand flashed out, catching him by the shoulder. Chris glanced at the larger boy, raising an eyebrow in question, but Sam only shook his head. Settling back in line, Chris glanced at Liz and saw his own confusion reflected in her eyes. Ashley's hand clenched around her wrist, holding her back.

The doctor glanced between the two groups, and with a shrug, pressed on. "Very well," he cleared his throat, "All of you, line up," he paused as the eight of them moved hesitantly to stand in one line, and then nodded. "Today—"

The doctor broke off, his brow creasing as the buzzer by the entrance sounded again. As one, the group turned towards the door. Chris shuddered as he glimpsed the face of the newcomer. Unconsciously he took a step back. A shiver ran through him, raising goose bumps down his arms and neck.

CHAPTER 10

CHRIS SHIVERED as Doctor Halt strode towards them, his eyes surveying the group as he approached. His arms swung casually at his sides, as though this were no more than a casual Sunday stroll for him. A smile played across his thin lips. He drew to a stop alongside the doctor that had been addressing them.

"Doctor Radly," his voice was like honey. "How goes training day?"

"Good," Radly spoke with hesitation. He was obviously surprised to see Halt. "How can I help you, sir?"

A soft laughter whispered from Halt's lips. "I thought I might assist," his eyes slid across the group of prisoners. "We need to advance our schedule – the directors are demanding results."

Radly bit his lips, eying them uncertainly. "We have four candidates ready in this unit. We still need time to assess the remaining four. Most of the other units are the same."

Shaking his head, Halt strode down the line, his eyes sweeping over each of them in turn. As Halt passed him, Chris risked a glance at the others. Sam and Ashley stared straight ahead, steadfastly ignoring the presence of Richard and Jasmine beside them. A hint of perspiration shimmered from Sam's brow, but otherwise the two of them seemed untouched by the run. On his other side, Liz stood with arms folded, while beyond the two newcomers wore uncertain frowns on their faces.

The crunch of gravel warned Chris of Halt's return, and he quickly turned to face straight ahead again. The man's eyes stared hard at Chris as he passed, and then moved on to Liz. The thud of his boots continued down the line as he went on to examine Joshua and William, before returning.

Scowling, Halt stood beside Doctor Radly. Raising an arm, he pointed at Liz, then to the lanky boy from the other group. "Those two," he scowled. "Pitiful creatures if ever I saw them. They won't last long."

Radly opened his mouth, then closed it. Glancing at his e-tablet, he shook his head and looked back at Halt. "Sir, we have a framework in place…" he trailed off as Halt stared at him.

Silence fell across the group of doctors. Chris glanced sideways at Liz, his heart beating hard against his chest. The girl stood staring straight ahead, her brow creased, fists clenched at her side. Though she did not move an inch, Chris could sense the tension building in her tiny frame, like a cat preparing to spring.

"Well, let's see," Halt's voice came again. A second later he strode past and stopped in front of Liz. "Elizabeth Flores," he looked her up and down. "How good to see you again."

Liz didn't move, just stood staring straight ahead. Nodding, Halt moved onto his next victim. "William Beth, a sorry looking excuse for a man, if ever I saw one."

A tremor went through the boy as he stepped back and raised his arms. "Please, sir, please, I'll do whatever you say."

Halt took another step forward, and the boy stumbled backwards. His feet slipped in the dust and he crashed to the ground. Towering over him, Halt sneered. "Pathetic," he spat. "Get up."

William nodded. He scrambled to his feet, eyes wide with terror. "Please—"

His plea was cut off as Halt's hand flashed out and caught him by the throat. Without apparent effort, the doctor hoisted the boy into the air. William gave a half-choked scream, his face darkening. His hands batted at Halt's arm, his legs kicking feebly in the air, but Halt did not waver. His cold grey eyes watched as the boy's struggles slowly grew weaker.

Chris watched in horror, his mouth open in a silent scream. A voice in his head screamed for him to help, but as he shifted an iron hand shot out and caught him by the wrist. He glanced back, opening his mouth to argue, but looking at Sam's face, the words died on his tongue. There was a cold despair in Sam's brown eyes, a haggard look to his face. Slowly, he shook his head.

Turning back, Chris watched as Halt tossed William to the ground. A low groan came from the boy as he struck, his legs collapsing beneath him. Dust billowed out around him. Gasping for breath, he struggled to his hands and knees and tried to crawl away.

Halt followed him at a casual stroll. Without taking his eyes from the boy, he began to speak. "You are all here at my pleasure. But I have no use for the weak," apparently losing patience with his victim, he lifted a foot and drove his boot into the small of his back. William collapsed face first into the ground.

Lifting his boot, Halt stared down at the boy. "Get up."

Arms shaking, William managed to lift himself to his hands and knees. His beet-red face looked up at Halt, eyes watering. He swayed where he crouched and a tremor went through him, but he made no move to stand.

Shaking his head, Halt growled. "Wretched speci-men. Well, if you're too lazy to stand, I will give you one last chance to prove your merit. How many pushups can you do?"

A confused look came over the boy's face. "Push… pushups?"

"Yes." Halt took a step closer, his face darkening.

William shook his head. "I… I don't know…"

Halt sucked in a breath. He turned to face the other doctors. "He doesn't know." He gave a soft laugh and turned back to the boy. "Well, shall we find out then?"

He stared down at the boy, waiting for a reply, but William had gone quiet. The eyes of every doctor and prisoner were on him. Chris held his breath, sensing the trap in Halt's tone, but not knowing how it would be sprung.

"Well, get to it then," Halt snapped. He looked up at the doctor hovering nearby. "Radly, you can call the count for us."

At Halt's feet, a sharp sob came from William. Slowly, he lowered his hands to the ground and spread his legs. As Radly shouted out the count, William lowered himself to within an inch of the ground and then straightened his arms again.

Chris and the others watched on, faces grim, as Radly continued to count. Beside him, Liz's expression was unreadable, though there was a slight sheen to her eyes, hinting at tears.

As Radly reached fifteen, William's arms began to tremble. His breath came in ragged gasps and his face flushed red. A shudder ran through his bony body, and with a sob he collapsed to the ground. A triumphant grin spread across Halt's face as he folded his arms.

"Sixteen," Radly repeated the call.

"Please," William coughed, lying with limbs splayed across the ground, "please, please I can't!"

"Keep going," Halt snarled.

He tried, Chris had to give him that. Veins popping in his forehead, teeth clenched, arms shaking with the effort, the boy managed half a pushup before he collapsed back to the ground. This time he didn't bother to beg, just lay staring up at Halt, a haunted look in his eyes.

Shaking his head, Halt looked across at them. "In case you were wondering, this is what 'weak' looks like." Cold eyes still watching them, Halt reached down and tapped the sleek black glass of his watch.

Chris flinched as an awful scream came from the ground. He stumbled backwards, turning to face the source, raising his fists to defend himself. But there was no threat – just William, thrashing on the ground, his half-gasped screams clawing their way up from his throat. Eyes wide and staring, William's head slammed back against the ground. His fingers bent into claws, scrambling at the steel collar around his neck, even as another convulsion tore through him.

Panic gripped Chris and he stepped towards the boy. Sam's iron grasp stopped him again, pulling him back. Chris swore, struggling to break free, unable to stand by and watch the torture any longer. He looked at Sam, fighting to break free, but Sam only stared passed him, eyes never leaving the convulsing boy. Behind him, Ashley stood as still as a statue, her eyes fixed on William, her face expressionless. Her scarlet hair blew across her face, but she did not so much as raise a hand to brush it away.

The fight went from Chris in a rush. Shuddering with horror, he turned back.

"Such a shame, to see our people come to this," Halt's words slithered through the air, filled with contempt. "Once upon a time we were proud, strong. Our forefathers marched to war with joy in their hearts and sent the cowards of the United States scurrying. Even then they did not stop. They followed the enemy back to their holes, and left a smoking crater in the heart of their so-called democracy."

Chris gritted his teeth. Beside Halt, William's struggles were weakening, his eyes closing as the veins on his neck stood taught. Agony swept across his features, contorting his face into a twisted scowl.

Still Halt spoke. "How your ancestors would turn in their graves to know of your treachery, of your betrayal of the nation they fought to create."

Forcing his eyes closed, Chris sucked in a breath. The hand on his shoulder gave a gentle squeeze, but otherwise Sam stayed silent. Through the strangled screams, Halt's words twisted their way through Chris's ears. The wrinkled, smiling face of his grandmother drifted through his mind, telling of how her husband had fought and died in the American war. In 2020, a conglomerate of Washington, Oregon and California had unilaterally ceded from the United States. Arizona and New Mexico had quickly joined them, as support poured in from Canada and Mexico.

For a few years, a tense peace had hovered between the newly formed Western Allied States and the USA. However, talks had quickly descended to threats, as the USA demanded their return to the union. Within a few years, war was declared, and chaos had engulfed North America. A decade of conflict followed, leaving thousands dead on both sides.

Then, as the war was coming to a head, the Western Allied States had made one last, desperate gamble. In one decisive strike, Washington, DC was left in ruins, the leadership of the United States demolished in a single blow. The remnants of the union quickly crumbled then, leaving a scattering of independent states who either signed for peace, or were overrun.

Many scholars argued the values and beliefs of both nations had been lost the day Washington, DC fell. The Western Allied States had been left tainted, their ideals corrupted by that one act of evil. Watching Halt torture the helpless boy, Chris could not help but agree.

"Perhaps some of you may prove worthy, may one day live up to the memories of your ancestors." Halt's eyes flashed as he watched them.

Biting back a scream, Chris tensed his fists. More than anything he wanted to wipe the smirk from the doctor's face. Only Sam's firm hand on his shoulder stopped him.

Halt stared down at the boy, arms folded. The light on William's collar still flashed red, though his twitching had slowed to little jerks of his arms and legs. He let out a long sigh. "I will give the boy this, he does not die easily," he reached for his watch.

"*Halt*," Halt froze as a woman's voice carried across the dirt.

The group turned as one, staring as Doctor Fallow

strode through the entrance. Chris blinked. So engrossed had he been in William and Halt, he had not heard the buzz of her entrance. Now, as she marched across the dusty ground, Fallow tapped at the watch on her wrist. Beside Halt, William's convulsions came to a sudden stop.

For a moment, Chris thought the boy had finally succumbed to the collar. Then a low groan came from his twisted body, and Chris let out a sigh of relief. He looked across as Fallow drew to a stop in front of Halt, her eyes flashing with anger.

"What the *hell* do you think you're doing?" Fallow growled.

CHAPTER 11

"WHAT THE *HELL* do you think you're doing?" Angela Fallow growled, her heart pounding as Halt turned to face her.

"My job." Halt's eyes flashed, and Angela took an involuntary step backwards.

Shaking her head at her weakness, Angela drew herself up. "Your job is to oversee this facility, Halt. Mine is to ensure we have the candidates needed for the project." Her eyes flickered to the boy lying at Halt's feet, and her stomach swirled.

The boy lay unconscious on the ground, an angry red spreading around his throat like a rash. He gave the odd twitch as his muscles spasmed, but otherwise he was still, the only sign of life the dull rattling of his breath. It looked like she had arrived just in time. One of the doctors had alerted her to Halt's interference with his tablet, but she had been on the other side of the facility.

Halt took a step towards her, his fists clenched. "Need I remind you, Fallow, you answer to me."

This time Angela did not back down. She lifted her head, facing the taller doctor. "Not in this, Halt. The Praegressus project is *mine* to oversee. Its framework was designed by all of us; we *all* agreed to follow it while vetting the candidates," she twisted her lips. "However distasteful some of us may consider the methods."

Taking another step, Halt towered over her. His eyes burned with rage, and for a long moment, he did not speak. She stared him down, unwilling to break, to give in. Halt had gone too far, stepped a mile past the lines of human decency here. Whoever their prisoners were, they did not deserve to be treated like this.

The breath went from Halt in a sudden rush. Nodding he waved a hand and turned away. "Very well, Fallow," he said the words lightly, but she did not miss the warning beneath them. He turned towards the watching doctors. "We shall do things *your* way. But we cannot wait. I want the new round of trials started tomorrow. The final batch of candidates will be needed by the week's end."

Swallowing, Angela glanced at her co-workers. They hovered in a group, a mixture of fear and disdain in their eyes. She knew some would support her, eager to do things by the book. But others she was not so sure on. They were more willing to take risks, to press on without concern for the candidates brought to the facility. Or they were just plain terrified of Halt.

In truth, she could not blame them. While she had once regarded the man with respect, since his elevation to head doctor, he had revealed a darker side. Doctors who crossed him were terminated without cause, safety procedures had been cut, and with the subjects, there were no limits to his cruelty.

She eyed him now, silently calculating the population of subjects still to be vetted. There were two hundred prisoners in the facility, with roughly half of them still needing to confront the parameters of the framework. That left a hundred candidates to vet – of which fifty would hopefully survive to begin the experiment.

And that wasn't even accounting for the final touches she needed to make on the formula.

"A week's not enough time," she said.

Halt shrugged. "I'm sorry, Fallow. That's out of my hands. The directors want results. The people are growing restless, they need answers, and if the government doesn't provide them…" he trailed off.

Angela sucked in a breath, her eyes travelling over the group of prisoners in their orange jumpsuits. She shivered as she met the boy's eyes. Christopher stared back at her, eyes wide, the unspoken question written across his face.

She quickly looked away, hearing again the screams of the boy's mother. Biting her lip, she faced Halt. "We'll have to skip the resting period. It may result in sub-optimal outcomes."

Halt waved a hand. He was already moving towards the doorway, leaving his tortured victim lying face down in the dust. "You will find a solution, Fallow," their eyes met, "I know you will."

Angela's breath caught in her throat, but she held his gaze until he turned away. She shuddered as he disappeared through the iron doors, the resistance falling from her like water. A half-muffled groan slipped from her lips, but she bit it back and turned towards the gathered doctors.

They stared back at her, awaiting instruction.

Angela straightened. "Okay, you heard Halt. We need to get these candidates classified. You know the drill." She clapped her hands and smiled as the other doctors broke from their silent reverie.

One by one, the doctors moved away, each taking one of the orange-garbed candidates with them. She saw Radly take the boy, Christopher, by the arm, saw his hazel eyes turn in her direction. Looking away, she studied a cloud drifting through the sky. Her mind drifted for a moment, remembering again the way Margaret Sanders had fought. The woman had downed a highly-trained Marine, almost killed him in fact.

A mother's love.

Idly, she remembered her own mother, the way she had fussed over their little family. Despite the wide expanse of the property, they had always struggled, making do with the rations the landowner left for them. But her mother had suffered their poverty with good grace, stewing rabbit bones and baking hard bread in the coal stove.

She imagined Margaret Sanders possessed a

similar resolve, a determination to do what was best for her children.

So why, then, had she been so foolish. Her treason against the government had doomed her son, and only by the grace of the government had he not been tossed into an interrogation cell alongside her. She shuddered, thinking of those dark places, imagining the woman's pretty face bruised and beaten.

Out on the field, Chris had begun to run, as Doctor Radly studied readings on his tablet. The collars transmitted a constant stream of data to the tablets: heartbeat, blood pressure, oxygen levels, and a range of other readings. That information would be used to rank them later.

Watching the candidates, Angela turned her thoughts to what lay ahead for them. She shuddered as a darkness settled on her soul. Again, she reminded herself what was at stake, of the necessity of the Praegressus project. Again, she could not quite convince herself.

CHAPTER 12

LIZ LAY IN THE DARKNESS, eyes open, staring out into empty space. Somewhere above was the concrete ceiling, but in the pitch-black she imagined the sky stretched overhead, infinite in its expanse. Only there were no stars, no moon or drifting satellites, and in her heart, she could not convince herself of the illusion.

In her heart, she remained trapped, locked away within the soulless walls of the facility.

She could still feel the boy's eyes watching her, begging for help, for an end to the torture. A shudder ran through her as she remembered the way Halt had looked at her, the piercing grey of his eyes as he considered her worth. It had been so close, a simple coin toss, and he might have chosen her…

Biting back a sob, Liz closed her eyes, though it made no difference in the darkness. She had wanted to go to him; only Ashley's hand had stopped her.

Instead, she had stood in silence, hand in hand with the girl from the city, as William slid towards death.

In the cell, Liz shivered, a scream building in her throat. She bit it back, and drew the thin cover closer. Goosebumps pricked at her skin as she rolled onto her side. Her body ached and a constant thud came from her temples. The doctors had subjected them to eight hours of torturous exercise, until the sun had finally dropped below the towering walls. By then her body had been little more than a series of bruises. A measly meal of broiled stew had followed in their cell, though in truth it was better than most of what she'd scavenged on the streets. Then the lights had clanked off, plunging them into the darkness.

"You okay, Liz?" Ashley whispered from the darkness.

Liz suppressed a shudder.

Am I okay? She turned the question over in her mind. Silently, she wondered whether she would ever be okay again. At the thought, a yearning rose within her, a need for companionship, for comfort.

"I'm alive," she replied, then. "What about you?"

Out on the field, Ashley had barely moved while William lay writhing in the dirt. Her face had remained impassive, the only sign anything was amiss was her iron-like grip around Liz's hand. Afterwards, Ashley had moved through the drills and tasks set by the doctors with an eerie calm, as though her mind were far away, detached from the horrors around her.

There was a long pause before Ashley replied.

"I'm alive too." Her breath quickened. "That's saying a lot."

"How long... how long have you and Sam been here?"

Another pause. "Weeks, a month. I've lost count of the days."

"And... And you've seen things like that, like today with William?"

Below, Ashley gave a sharp snort. "That, and worse." She shifted in the bed, causing the bunk to rock. "It only gets worse, Liz."

Liz shivered, thinking of the icy glances that had passed between Ashley and Sam, and the couple in the other group. "What about the two in the other group, Richard and Jasmine and the rest."

"What about them?" Ashley's response was abrupt, her voice sharp.

"You knew them," Liz whispered softly, aware she was treading on dangerous ground. "Or at least, you knew Richard and Jasmine."

"You'll find out soon enough, Liz. Best you not worry about it."

Liz swallowed. Ashley's reply brooked no argument, and an uneasy silence fell between them. For a while, Liz lay still, staring into space, wondering at the truth behind Ashley's words. Below, Sam gave a snort and rolled in his bed. Liz stifled a groan as a rumble came from the boy's chest and he started to snore.

"The boys don't seem to be having any trouble sleeping," she whispered, hoping Ashley was still awake.

"You know what boys are like," came Ashley's reply. She could almost hear the girl smiling. "Emotional capacity of a brick and all…" her voice trailed off for a moment. "Sam… he closes it off I think, buries it deep. It comes out in other ways though, his frustration. Like how he reacted to Chris when you arrived."

"And you?" Liz couldn't help but dig deeper. Through the heat and torture, the agonising exercise and the hard-faced stares of the doctors, Ashley had not missed a beat. She had smiled through each new challenge, as though privy to some secret joke, and moved with that same fluid grace Liz had first seen displayed in this cell.

When the girl did not answer, Liz pressed on. "You looked so calm, even when…" she trailed off as William's agonised face flashed through her thoughts.

Ashley had remained impassive throughout it all, only moving once Doctor Fallow arrived to intervene. Her calm had been… frightening.

"I was?" Ashley sounded surprised. Sheets rustled in the darkness. "I wasn't. Inside I was screaming, but I've learned when to keep things to myself, when not to draw attention. Even before this place, it was a skill I'd mastered."

Liz sat up at that. "What do you mean?"

Soft laughter came from below. "I've had a lot of practice, Liz. My parents worked for the government."

An icy hand slid its way down Liz's throat and wrapped its fingers around her heart. Her breath stuttered, the cold steel pressing against her throat. She grasped at the covers, fingers tearing at the cheap fabric.

Below, Ashley was still talking. "They worked in Media Relations, of all things. No one important, nothing to do with the President and his people. Just a couple of analysts in a tiny department of our fine administration," her last sentence rang with sarcasm. "But even two lowly analysts quickly discovered there's no such thing as free speech these days. *Especially* for those close to power. They had to learn to wear masks, to hide their true beliefs about the goings-on of the government. By the time my older sister and I came along, they were masters at it. So I guess you could say, I learned from the best."

"Why would they stay?" Liz tried to hide it, but the question came out harsh, accusing.

A ruffle of blankets came from below her. "Why?" Ashley's voice trailed off, as though considering the question. "For us, I guess. To give us a better life. They may not have agreed with everything the government did, but they knew leaving was not really an option. Their careers would have been destroyed. They didn't want to raise their daughters on the streets."

"Yes, it's not much of a life," Liz all but growled.

Ashley fell silent, and for a long while it seemed she would not reply. Guilt welled in Liz's chest, but she pushed it down. Anger wound its way around her throat, but before she could reply, Ashley spoke.

"Didn't really matter in the end though, did it?

They sacrificed their beliefs, their integrity, so we could live, but it didn't make any difference. They were found out, and here I am."

Liz's anger dwindled with Ashley's words. It was not the girl's fault she had been born into wealth, while Liz had been condemned to the poverty-stricken regions. Even so, she could not quite set aside the anger, could not quite let it go.

"Sorry," she offered at last, her tone still harsh. "It's just, for as long as I can remember, the government has been the enemy. Even as a child, they were the people who came and took our food, the landowners who held our lives in the palm of their hands. Then, when I was older, after my parents… after they passed…" She shook her head, angry images flashing through her mind.

"I understand," Ashley's whisper came from below. "But none of that matters now, does it? Whatever our parents were, whatever we've been through, we've arrived at the same destiny. We're both trapped in the same nightmare. You'll learn that, soon enough."

"It gets worse?" Liz spoke the words without emotion. Her energy was spent, and she could hardly bring herself to care about whatever new trials the morning might hold.

"Only if you're human," Ashley replied.

The words rang with finality and Liz sensed the conversation had come to an end. Shivering, she hugged the covers tight around her. Suddenly she longed to be wrapped in another's arms, felt the need for human touch. An image of her mother drifted through her thoughts, a warm smile on her lips, eyes dancing with humour.

Biting back a sob, Liz buried her head in the pillow, anxious to hide her sorrow. As she cried, another thought drifted through her thoughts, a question that demanded an answer. One she should have asked. Silently, she cursed her selfish grief.

"Ashley," she breathed. "What happened to your sister?"

Silence hung over the darkness, and long minutes passed, until Liz was sure the girl had already fallen asleep.

"She's dead." The answer came just as Liz was preparing to give up.

The girl's soft sobs carried up from below, carrying with them the pain of loss.

"I'm sorry," Liz whispered, the words hollow, even to her.

Ashley did not reply, and Liz lay back on her bed, listening as the girl's sobs faded away.

It was a long time before sleep found Liz.

CHAPTER 13

LIZ STUMBLED as she entered the room, the sudden, brilliant light blinding her. Stars danced across her vision as the door slammed closed behind her. She jumped at the sound, and almost tripped, before she managed to right herself. Straightening, she blinked again and looked around the room.

Overhead, fluorescent bulbs lined the ceiling, filling the room with their distant whine. Otherwise, the room was unlike anything she'd seen so far. Three walls were covered by white padding, while the third shone with silver glass, its surface reflecting her tangled hair and shadowed eyes. She shivered, seeing the exhaustion in her eyes, the bruises marking her cheeks.

For three days, the doctors had taken them to the outdoor field, and driven them through an endless series of tests and exercise. Unused to the constant strain, Liz had quickly learned that failure meant pain. So she had dug deep within herself, to stores of strength she had not known she possessed, and survived. But now things had changed again.

She took another step into the room, the soft floor yielding beneath her feet. Turning from the one-way mirror, she shifted to face the boy in the centre of the room. His long blond hair hung in dirty clumps around his face, where purple bruises matched Liz's own. Biting his lip, his eyes flickered around the room, uncertainty writ in his every movement. Behind him was another door, its surface padded like the one she had entered through.

Joshua, she recalled his name from their first day on the training field.

His eyes turned on her as she thought his name. "What's going on?" he croaked.

Liz shrugged and shook her head. "I don't know, Joshua."

They had not spoken since that first day on the field. Ashley and Sam had been insistent, refusing to even acknowledge the other group of inmates. Somehow, Liz did not think their rule applied now.

Before either of them could speak further, a loud squeal interrupted. Liz winced, the hairs on her neck standing up, before the sound died away. A voice quickly followed.

"Welcome," the voice began, coming from somewhere in the ceiling. "Congratulations on surviving the framework. As you know, only the strongest are needed for the final stages of the Praegressus project."

Liz crossed her arms and turned to face the mirror. Raising an eyebrow, she rolled her eyes so those behind could see. She was sick of listening to these people, to them acting like they owned her. Collar or no, she refused to be treated like an animal any longer, to bend to their will.

The voice ignored her display of insolence and continued. "Unfortunately, time constraints require us to press on. This phase of the project must be completed by week's end. This means omitting the standard rest period for new subjects such as yourselves."

"Hardly seems fair," Liz muttered under her breath, flashing a quick grin at Joshua.

Joshua shrugged and cast another uncertain look at the glass. They stood in silence for a moment, waiting for the voice to continue. "Regretfully, we must cull our population of candidates for the next phase of the Praegressus project. Only those with the strongest constitutions would survive the final process regardless, and we do not have resources to waste on failed specimens. Thus, today only the best will survive."

Liz shuddered at the way the voice described cold-blooded murder. She recalled the faces lining the corridor outside their cell. Some of those boys and girls could have been as young as thirteen, the oldest maybe twenty. Their whole lives were ahead of them. And these people wished to snuff them out, to cull them like they were no more than field mice beneath their boots.

Joshua seemed a little younger than her, maybe seventeen at a stretch. He was a little taller too, and bulkier, with the broad shoulders of a swimmer. His amber eyes were watching her now, his fear shining out like a beacon.

"Only one of you will leave that room alive. You must decide for yourselves, whether you possess the will to live. To the victor, goes life."

Liz clenched her fists, eyes flickering from the mirror to Joshua. She sought out some sign of the watchers beyond, but the glass was too thick, showing only the horror on her face. And the boy's wide eyes, the hardening of his brow, his fists clenching as he faced her.

Whatever her own thoughts, Joshua had clearly already made up his mind.

Only if you're human, Ashley's words from their midnight conversation returned to her.

They weighed on her soul as she watched Joshua, saw his muscles tensing. And she knew in her heart, she too would do whatever was necessary to survive.

The fear had already fallen from Joshua's face. His eyes swept over her, weighing her up. A smile spread across his lips as he realised his chances of victory were high. There was no question who the doctors expected to survive.

Straightening, he stepped towards her.

Liz quickly retreated. She studied him as they began to circle, searching for an advantage. It was easy to see she was no match for his strength, but she was light on her feet and hoped he might prove over-confident. After two years on the streets, wandering between towns and cities, Liz was no stranger to a fight.

Yet with the padded walls ringing her in, there was no room for mistakes. If he caught her in his long arms, she would be finished. Though she was yet to see how determined he was about his capacity for murder, she didn't want to test his mercy.

She certainly would not be giving him any second chances.

Joshua gave a sudden shout and leapt towards her, eating up the space between them in a single stride. Liz twisted as he came for her, jumping backwards to avoid his flailing arms, and smiled as he staggered past. Despite his size advantage, the boy was no fighter.

Maybe she stood a chance after all.

Joshua came to a stop near the wall and spun to face her. A wicked scowl twisted his face. Liz swallowed hard and braced herself.

Raising her fists, she nodded. "Let's get this over with then."

A low growl came from Joshua as he started towards her again, his footsteps controlled now, each movement carefully measured. Liz spread her feet wide and slid one foot backwards, readying herself. She had no intention of letting him get close enough to grab her, but he needed to be a *little* closer yet.

As Joshua took another step, Liz gave a low growl and hurled herself forward. His eyes widened as she closed in on him, but close as they were, there was no time to react. Liz slammed her fist into the centre of his chest, aiming for the solar plexus.

Air exploded between the boy's teeth and he staggered backwards, a half-choked groan rattling from his throat. The colour fled his face as he clutched his stomach, mouth wide and gasping.

Watching his distress, Liz hesitated, guilt welling up within her. Joshua had not been expecting her to fight back, certainly not with such sudden violence. But as he bent in two, wheezing in the cold air, she knew she could not spare him. If she allowed him to recover, he would not fall for the same trick again.

Bent in two, Joshua's head provided the perfect target. Stepping in, Liz clasped her hands together and brought them down on the back of his head.

Joshua's legs buckled and he slumped to the ground without a sound. His arms splayed out on either side of him and a muffled groan came from his mouth. Relief swept through Liz at the sound – at least she hadn't killed him. Maybe they would spare him. After all, they couldn't have expected her to win this matchup.

Turning to the one-way mirror, she raised an eyebrow in question. As she did, Joshua's hand shot out and grabbed her by the leg.

Liz screamed as fingers like steel closed around her ankle and tugged, sending her crashing to the ground. The shock of the fall sent the breath rushing from her, and she gasped, struggling to breathe. Pain shot through her ankle as the fingers squeezed. Screaming a curse, she kicked out with her foot, but

Joshua surged forward and caught it in his other hand.

Panic clenched Liz's stomach as she fought to break his grip. Sucking in a lungful of air, she tried to roll away, but his hands held her like iron shackles. However hard she strained, he held her tighter, teeth flashing as his lips drew back in a grin.

In a sudden rush, he dragged her across the floor, pulling himself up as he did so. For a second the hands released her, but before she could squirm free, Joshua's weight crashed down on her chest, pinning her down.

Hands fumbled at her throat, fingernails tearing at her skin.

Tendrils of horror wrapped around Liz and she lashed out with a fist, catching Joshua in the side of the head. He reeled sideways, but his weight did not shift and she failed to break free.

Recovering his balance, Joshua snarled and raised a fist. Flinching, Liz raised her arm, then screamed as his blow glanced off her forearm and into her shoulder. She swung at his face again, but there was no strength in the blow this time, and it bounced weakly off his chin.

Liz was not so lucky.

Stars exploded across her vision as Joshua's fist connected with her forehead. Her head thudded back into the soft ground. Distantly she thought how kind it was for the doctors to have provided a padded floor while they murdered each other. Then another blow thudded into her jaw, and the fight went from her in a sudden rush. Darkness spun at the edges of her vision.

Cold fear spread through her stomach as an almost tentative hand wrapped around her neck. She sucked in a breath as pressure closed around her throat. Panic caught her as she stared up at Joshua, silently pleading for mercy.

Joshua stared back, eyes hard, lips drawn back in a snarl. His teeth clenched with rage – whoever he'd been before entering this room, that Joshua was now long gone. He had been burned away, the innocence of the boy replaced by anger, by bitter hatred, and the desperation to live.

Fire grew in Liz's chest, willing her to action. She kicked feebly, struggling to manoeuvre herself into a position to attack. But his weight was far beyond her strength to lift, and before she could struggle further he lifted her head and slammed it back into the ground. Despite the spongy surface, Liz's head spun.

She opened her mouth, gasping in desperation, but the pressure did not relent. Darkness filled the edges of her vision as every muscle in her body began to scream. Bit by bit her strength slipped away, replaced by the endless burning of suffocation.

On top of her, Joshua leaned closer, eyes wide with vicious intent.

In that moment, Liz saw her chance.

He was so close, just inches away. She could not miss. With the last of her strength, she clenched her fist and drove it up into Joshua's throat. The steel rim of the collar bit into her knuckles, but behind it, she felt something give, something fracture with the force of her blow.

The pressure around her throat vanished as Joshua toppled backwards. A low gurgling echoed off the walls as he gasped, his hands going to his own neck, his legs thrashing against the soft floor.

Liz sucked in a long gasp of icy air, her throat burning as air flooded her lungs. A wave of agony swept through her, but she struggled to her hands and knees, still coughing and wheezing. Her head swirled and the room spun, but she dug her nails into the spongy floor and willed herself to remain conscious.

Get up, Liz!

Summoning the last of her strength, Liz pulled herself to her feet and stood swaying in the centre of the room. The white lights burned in her eyes, blinding her, but she clenched her fists, and by sheer will stayed upright.

She looked down at Joshua, bracing herself, and her stomach lurched.

Joshua no longer moved, no longer thrashed, no longer breathed. His mouth hung open, his eyes wide and staring, but the boy was gone. His face was a mottled white and purple, the veins of his neck bulging, and a black bruise was already spreading from beneath his collar.

Joshua lay dead at her feet, his life fled.

Tears ran from Liz's eyes as she sank to the ground.

The darkness came rushing up to meet her.

CHAPTER 14

CHRIS WATCHED as William staggered upright, his heart sinking at the thought of another round. But to his relief, the boy's feet slipped from beneath him and he toppled forward, landing with an undignified thud on the padded floor.

Closing his eyes, Chris let out a long sigh.

It's over.

The thought offered scant comfort. In truth, it had not been much of a fight. While William was tall and had long arms, there was not a scrap of muscle on the boy. And he had never quite recovered from the first day on the field. Young and inexperienced, he had still been the first to attack, but it was clear his heart was not in it. Chris had easily deflected his clumsy blows and retreated across the room.

Crossing his arms, he had looked at the glass, and shaken his head in refusal.

A loud beep had come from his collar followed by a bolt of electricity that sent him to his knees. Gasping, he reached for the steel collar, but the shock had already ceased.

The voice had come again as Chris climbed back to his feet.

"That was your only warning. Engage with your opponent, or forfeit your life."

That had been five minutes ago, and despite his reluctance, Chris had had no choice but to obey.

Now guilt ate at his stomach, curdling the measly remnants of his breakfast. William crouched on the floor, his breath coming in ragged gasps as he struggled to regain his feet.

Despite the voice's command, Chris had still held back, pulling his blows where he could. But as the fight progressed, the boy had grown more desperate, and Chris had been forced to act.

A kick to William's head had sent him reeling, and he had never recovered.

Now Chris waited, staring into the mirrored glass, struggling to pierce the reflection and find the faces of his captors. Whoever they were, he hated them with a violence he had not thought himself capable of.

The door behind the boy opened with a squeal of old hinges. Chris looked up as two guards entered, followed by a woman in a white lab coat. His heart lurched, before he realised the woman was not Fallow. One of the guards moved across to check on William, while the other approached Chris, gesturing him back against the wall.

Once she was satisfied both prisoners were secure, the woman strode across the room, her lips pursed, eyes fixed on the fallen boy. A wireless headset curled around her left ear, half hidden by the curls of her auburn hair. She spoke as she moved, transmitting observations to whoever was on the other end. In one hand, she carried a sleek steel instrument.

Chris shivered as he recognised the gun-shaped jet injector, identical to the one Fallow had used on him the night he was taken.

The woman who was not Fallow crouched beside William, still talking into her headset. William was on his hands and knees, struggling to find his balance. Reaching out, the woman laid a hand on his shoulder.

"Subject is still conscious. He appears to be suffering from concussion," her words carried across to Chris. "Assessment?"

A low groan came from William as he turned towards the woman's voice. "Wha... what happened?"

Chris closed his eyes, guilt welling up within him. He had seen these same symptoms in his Dojang, when younger fighters failed to wear their head guards. Still, he didn't think he'd hit William too hard, just enough to take the fight out of him.

The doctor was nodding to the voice in her ear. "Affirmative. There would be no purpose in resuming the fight. Administering the injection."

Before Chris could react to the announcement, the woman leaned down and pressed the jet injector to William's neck. The hiss of gas followed as the vial attached to the gun emptied. Quickly, she withdrew the gun, stood, and retreated across the room.

On the ground, William raised a hand to his neck, his face tightening.

The woman looked on, face impassive, arms crossed and fingers tapping against her elbow.

Whatever had been in the injection did not take long to act. Chris stood frozen as William began to cough. Then, without warning his eyes rolled back in his skull. A violent shudder went through him as his breathing stopped, then began again with a desperate gasp, as though he were sucking air through a straw. He bent over, groaning, his mouth moving as he tried to speak. Wild eyes flickered around the room, pleading for help.

As William's desperate eyes found Chris, the spell broke. He started forward, but the outstretched arm of a guard barred his way. Before he could slip past, the guard grasped him by the shirt and tossed him back against the wall. The pads broke the impact, but he staggered as he landed and barely kept his feet.

He looked up in time to see William pitch face first into the ground, a low moan marking his final exhalation of breath. His feet kicked for a second, then lay still. Silence fell across the room as the guard stepped back from Chris and faced the doctor.

The woman walked across the room and crouched beside William. Reaching out, she felt his neck. After a few seconds, she gave a curt nod.

"Subject has expired. Subject Christopher Sanders has passed the framework," her voice was cold.

"*Why?*" Chris screamed.

The woman looked up quickly, her eyes widening. Beside her, the guards edged forwards, placing themselves between Chris and the doctor.

"Why?" Chris grated again, taking a step forward.

The woman's surprise had already faded, though her eyes flicked to the guards before she addressed him. "He was weak. He would not have survived phase two. This was the humane option."

"*Humane?*" Chris clenched his fists. "He was helpless!"

"With the concussion, he would have passed without pain," the doctor spoke with a calm efficiency, as though explaining something to a child.

A wild anger took Chris then, an impossible rage that swept away all caution. Without thinking, he leapt forward, fingers reaching for the woman's throat. The guards stepped forward to meet him, but Chris never made it that far.

Agony tore through his neck, spreading in an instant through every fibre of his being, taking his feet out from under him. He gasped as he struck the ground, his arms locking, every muscle screaming as a thousand needles stabbed them. A convulsion rippled through him and his limbs flailed wildly. His head thumped hard against the ground, as the reek of burning reached his nostrils. His back arched and he opened his mouth to unleash a silent scream.

When the agony finally ceased, he found himself staring up at the ceiling. The bright light sent a bolt of agony through his head, and he quickly closed his eyes again.

Movement came from nearby, followed by a voice. "Do that again, and we will find someone else to fill your place."

Chris opened his eyes to find the woman crouched beside him. She held a finger over her watch, a ready smile twisting her lips.

He nodded, swallowing hard as the collar pressed against his throat.

"This is for the greater good, Christopher," the doctor continued. "Without us, you would all be in the same place as this boy. At least here, we have given you a fighting chance. Trust me, when I say the government interrogators are not nearly as humane."

She stood then, waving a hand at the guards. "Get him up."

Rough hands grasped Chris beneath his shoulders and hauled him to his feet. He stumbled as they held him, struggling to control his legs. They jerked and twitched, refusing to obey, but eventually he got them firmly on the ground. Even so, the guards did not release him, perhaps knowing from experience how unstable he was.

"Bring him," the woman said as she turned and opened the door.

Chris's eyes lingered on the dead boy as the guards dragged him from the room. William still lay where he had fallen, still and silent, eyes wide and staring from the lifeless husk of his body.

Then they were outside, marching down long white corridors. Distantly, Chris thought they were heading for the cells, but he paid no attention to his surroundings. His mind was elsewhere, locked away in the room with William, his dead eyes still staring.

It's your fault, the thought ate at him.

William had never stood a chance. The minute they'd entered the room, the boy's life had been forfeit. These people had known it, had wanted it to happen.

Doors slammed as they moved deeper into the facility. He knew where they were heading now, that he would soon find himself back in the tiny cell. The others would be waiting for him. And they would know, would see the truth in his eyes.

That he was a killer.

CHAPTER 15

THE STEEL DOOR to the prison block appeared ahead, the guards already moving to open it. In a blink, they were through, marching down the long corridor of the prison block. The cells were almost empty now, only a few faces remaining to press against the bars and watch Chris's return.

When he first saw their cell, he thought it was empty. But as the guards drew the door open, he glimpsed movement from Liz's bed, saw her haggard face poke into view. She watched in grim silence as the guards propelled Chris inside.

Steel screeched behind him, followed by the clang of the locking mechanism. Footsteps retreated down the corridor, fading until another clang announced their departure.

Reaching out, Chris gripped the metal bar of his bunk. His legs shook, threating to give way. He closed his eyes, waiting for Liz to speak, to hurl her accusations.

You killed him.

The words whispered in his mind, but Liz remained silent. Only the distant tread of the guard in the corridor could be heard. He took a deep breath, tasting the bleach in the air, the blood from a cut on his lip.

"Are you okay?" He jumped as Liz finally spoke.

He looked up then, finding Liz's big eyes watching him, and saw his own pain reflected in their sapphire depths. She sat in her bunk, knuckles wide as she gripped the metal sidebar. Her eyes watered and a single tear streaked down her cheek.

"No." Chris's shoulders slumped. "You?"

She shook her head, looked away, but he had seen the flash of guilt in her eyes. The truth hung over the room like a blanket, smothering them.

They were alive.

Taking a better grip of his bunk, Chris hauled himself up. Dragging himself across the sagging mattress, he collapsed into his pillow. Then he turned and saw Liz still watching him. Her lips trembled. There was no sign of the proud, defiant girl he'd first seen in the cages. The last few days, last few hours, had broken her.

Broken us both, a voice reminded him.

Pushing himself up, Chris twisted to face Liz. "Did they…" his voice trailed off. He couldn't finish the question.

Her crystal blue eyes found his, shining in the glow of the overhead lights. "No," she whispered. "I did."

A chill went through Chris at her words. He stared at her, noticing now the purple bruise on her cheek, the dried blood on her lip. His eyes travelled lower and found the swollen black skin beneath her collar. He shuddered. Her struggle had been far more real than his. He remembered the boy Joshua, guessed he was the one…

"What happened?" he murmured.

Liz closed her eyes. "I didn't mean…" She sucked in a breath, and her eyes flashed open. "I didn't *want* to," she finished with a growl.

Chris nodded, leaning back against the concrete wall. "You did what you had to, Liz," he offered.

"He would have killed me," she continued as though he had not spoken. "I had to do it. He left me no choice…"

Chris felt a sudden urge to wrap his arms around the girl, to hold her until the pain left her. This was a side of her he had not seen, the vulnerability beneath the armour she'd worn from the first moment he'd laid eyes on her. Gone was the hardness, the distant air of superiority. The foulness of this place had eaten the rest, had reduced them both to shadows of their former selves.

He could almost feel his humanity fading away, slipping through his fingers like grains of rice. With each fresh atrocity he witnessed, with every awful thing they forced him to do, he could feel his soul slipping away, feel himself becoming the animal they thought him to be. One way or another, soon he would cease to exist, and nothing would remain of the boy his mother had raised.

"It doesn't matter." Liz looked up at that. He continued, his voice breaking. "Whether you killed him or not, only one of you was ever walking out of that room. After my... after William fell, the doctors came. He couldn't stand, couldn't defend himself. They executed him."

A sharp hiss of breath came from Liz, but it was a long time before she replied. "Who are these people?"

Monsters. Chris thought, but did not speak the word.

Across from him, Liz started to cough. A long, drawn out series of wheezes and gasps rattled from her chest, going on and on, until her face was flushed red and her brow creased with pain.

Finally, she leaned back against the wall, panting for breath.

"Are you okay?" Chris whispered

Liz opened her eyes and stared at him. "Of course, city boy. I can take a beating."

Chris winced. His own anger rose but he bit back a curt reply. There was no point taking offence. He could see her pain, knew where the anger came from. He had not missed the coldness with which she addressed them at times, her hesitation to join their conversations.

Another rattle came from her chest as she laid her head back against the wall.

"We're not all bad, you know," he said at last. "Not all rich, either. There are a lot of people who disagree with the government now, even in the cities. There have been protests…"

"Protests?" Liz coughed, her voice wry. "Well, nice to hear you're getting out."

Chris sighed. "I understand–"

"I don't think you do," Liz cut him off. "You think you do, but you don't. While you lived in your cosy home in the city, I was forced onto the streets. Not because I wanted to, not because I had a choice, but because everyone I knew was dead. Slaughtered."

Shivering, Chris opened his mouth to reply, then closed it, unable to find the words.

Liz eyed him for a moment and then continued. "I had nowhere to go, no one left to turn to. I thought the government would help when they arrived, that they would protect me. But when they came, they looked at me like I was nothing, like I was an inconvenience to them. They would have arrested me, thrown me in some place like this if I hadn't run."

Chris looked away from the pain in Liz's eyes. He stared at his hands, the bruises on his knuckles, his stomach clenched with guilt.

"I'm sorry," he whispered at last, looking up. "You shouldn't have been treated that way. It's not right," he paused. "Was it a *Chead*?"

Liz flinched at the word. When she did not reply, Chris went on. "Mum always said something needed to be done, that her father would have been ashamed by how things have changed since the war. We should never have let the inequality between the cities and the countryside grow so bad," he paused for breath,

"But that does not change what I said. We're not all evil, Liz. Some of us want to fix things, want the government to be held to account."

"So I should just give you all the benefit of the doubt?" Liz snapped.

"No," Chris replied in a soft tone. "You should judge us by our own actions, not those of others," he breathed out. "A long time ago, I might have hated you too, Liz. Feared you for being different, for speaking with a rural accent."

"But not now?"

He shook his head. "No," he trailed off, remembering a time long ago. "When I was younger, I was running late getting home from class. It was getting dark, and we don't live in a good neighbourhood. When I was nearly home, a man stepped from the shadows. He had a knife."

"Let me guess, he was from the country too?"

Chris laughed softly. "No, he spoke like a normal person." He couldn't help but tease her for the assumption. Shaking his head, he continued, "But I think he was an addict of some sort – his eyes were wild and his hands shook. Before I had a chance to reach for my bag, he swung the knife at me, and caught me in the shoulder. I still have the scar…"

Liz nodded. "I saw."

Chris glanced across at her, his cheeks warming. He remembered his embarrassment when they had been forced to remove their clothes. Apparently, Liz had allowed her eyes to roam more than his own.

"What does this have to do with anything, Chris?"

With a shrug, Chris continued. "I think he would have killed me if someone else hadn't come along." He paused, looking across at Liz. "I don't know where he came from, but suddenly there was a man standing between us. *He* spoke with a rural accent, told the mugger to leave. When the man didn't listen, my rescuer took his knife away and sent him running."

"And this suddenly changed your mind about us?"

Chris shrugged. "Not overnight, no. But the man walked me home, right to my front door. He even told mum what to do with my cut. He didn't have to help me, could have left me to die, dismissed me as some spoiled city boy who deserved it. But he chose to help me instead. Since then, I've tried to do the same. To give people a chance, whoever they are."

Liz let out a long sigh. "And you want the same from me now?" she asked. "Because some man from the country saved you from a mugger?"

Chuckling, Chris nodded his head. "It would be nice to have a clean slate."

Liz shook her head. "After today, I'm not sure a clean slate exists for us, Chris. Joshua's blood is on my hands…"

"No," Chris replied firmly. "It's on theirs."

Liz nodded, but they both knew the words meant little. They might not have had a choice, but that did not lessen the burden.

"We're all in this together now, aren't we?" Liz repeated Ashley's words from all those days ago, on the day they had arrived.

Chris's gut clenched as he realised the two still had not returned.

On the other bed, Liz continued, her voice hesitant. "Okay, Chris," she whispered. "I'll give you a chance."

"Thank you," he said after a while.

Silence settled around them again then. Chris stared up at the ceiling, struggling to resolve the conflict of emotion battling within him. William's face drifted through his thoughts, eyes wide and staring, but the guilt felt a little less now. Liz had faced the same question, given the same answer.

Somehow, that made things just a little easier to bear.

Long hours ticked past. Still the others did not return. Chris and Liz waited in the hushed stillness of the cell, listening to the thump of the guard's boots outside, the whisper of voices from other cells. Liz's breath grew more ragged.

Finally, the bang of the outer door announced someone's approach. The soft tread of footsteps followed, moving down the corridor. Metal screeched as cell doors opened, while other footsteps continued on towards them.

Chris sat up as shadows fell across the bars of their cell. Relief touched his chest as he looked out, and saw Ashley and Sam standing outside. Hinges squeaked as the door opened and they stumbled inside. Sad smiles touched their faces as they looked up at Chris and Liz.

"So," Sam breathed. "You're alive."

CHAPTER 16

WITHOUT PAUSING TO KNOCK, Angela shoved the door to Halt's office open and strode inside. She glimpsed surprise on the harsh lines of his face as he looked up, though it had vanished by the time the door slammed shut behind her. Anger replaced it as he half-rose from his chair, fists clenched hard on his desk.

"What—"

"You have no right!" Angela cut him off.

Halt straightened. "I have every right," his voice was low, dangerous.

Hands trembling, Angela approached his desk. "It's not ready, Halt," she hissed. "You can't start those trials tomorrow. I need more time."

Rising, Halt walked around his desk, until he stood towering over her. Angela stared back, defiant, anger feeding her strength. She had just learned Halt planned to initiate the next phase of the Praegressus project tomorrow. The same project she had dedicated the last ten years of her life too.

"The directors want results, Doctor Fallow," Halt bit out the words, "and you've been stalling."

Angela refused to back down. "I've been doing my job," she snapped. "And I'm telling you, *the virus is not ready!*"

Halt smiled. "I've looked over your work, Fallow," Angela shivered at his tone. "And I say it's ready. After all, *fortune favours the bold*."

The words of the old Latin proverb curled around Angela's mind as she stepped back. They reminded her of Halt in those first days. The government had sent him after her discovery with the *Chead*, bringing her their new directive.

The Praegressus Project.

Praegressus – Latin for evolution, the adaptation of species down the countless millennia.

Shivering, Angela drew in a breath to steady herself. "There are still problems with the uptake," she ground out. "You could kill them all with your recklessness."

"The alternations will work–"

"Of course they will," Angela interrupted. "Animal trials have shown us as much. It's their immune response that concerns me. Their bodies will tear themselves apart fighting the virus."

Halt waved a hand as he moved back behind his desk. "Should that eventuate, we will administer immunosuppressants until the chromosomal changes have set," he sat back at his desk, eyebrow raised. "Is that all?"

"Immunosuppressants?" Angela pressed her palms against the desk and leaned in. "We'll have to move them to the clean room, watch them around the clock. They wouldn't last a day in the cells."

"Whatever it takes, Fallow." Halt stared her down. "We can't wait any longer. The government wants answers. We'll be shut down if we don't provide a solution soon. The attacks are growing worse. The authorities are desperate."

"What?" Angela questioned.

Halt leaned back in his chair. "The fools underestimated the *Chead* for too long. They should have given us the funding we needed for this years ago. There was an attack in San Francisco yesterday. They've reached the capital, Fallow. The President himself is demanding answers."

Angela shook her head, doubt gnawing at her chest. "You really think this is the answer?"

"Of course." Halt's cold eyes regarded her with a detached curiosity. "Do not lose focus now, Doctor Fallow. Not when we're so close. The Praegressus project will change everything. When it succeeds, the Western Allied States will herald in a new era of human evolution. The *Chead* will be hunted down and eradicated, our enemies at home and abroad consigned to the pages of history."

Looking into her superior's eyes, Angela shuddered. Naked greed lurked in their grey depths. For the first time, she allowed herself to look around, to take in the grisly display lining the walls of Halt's office. The sight she had been doing her best to ignore.

All around, animal eyes stared back at her. Halt's office was lined with shelves, each holding a collection of jars filled with clear fluids. Suspended within hung a silent host of animals of every shape and size. Birds and lizards, cats and snakes and what looked like a platypus stared down at her, their eyes blank and dead. An opossum curled around its ringed tail on the shelf behind Halt's head, while beside it a baby chimpanzee hugged its chest. With its eyes closed, it could have been sleeping.

Angela looked away, struggling to hide her disgust from Halt.

"Soon they will all be obsolete," Halt commented, noticing her discomfort.

"Yes," she almost choked on the word.

But at what cost? She added silently.

Halt eyed her closely and raised one eyebrow. "Was there anything else, Doctor Fallow?"

Angela shook her head. She knew when she was defeated. Turning, she all but ran from the room. She closed the door carefully behind her, her anger spent. Once outside, she placed a hand against the wall, shivering with sudden fear. Events were accelerating now, slipping beyond her control, and it was all she could do to keep up.

In her mind, she saw images of San Francisco, the steep roads teaming with life. She imagined the devastation a *Chead* would cause in such a place, the mindless slaughter. Bodies would line the streets as police struggled to reach the scene through the traffic-clogged streets. How long might the *Chead* have run rampant?

Straightening, Angela turned from Halt's door and moved away. Tomorrow, if they succeeded, the world would change. Humanity's evolution would take one giant leap forward, and one way or another, there would be no going back.

A sudden doubt rose within her, a fear for what was to come. What if they were wrong? What if they failed, and it was all for nought?

And what if they succeeded? What then?

Her skin tingled as she remembered Halt's words, heard again his triumphant declaration.

Our enemies, at home and abroad, will be consigned to the pages of history.

CHAPTER 17

A COLD BREEZE blew across Liz's neck, rustling the branches above her head. Sucking in a breath, she picked up the pace, eying the lengthening shadows beneath the trees. She was close to home now, the path familiar beneath her feet, but it was a steep climb and she had no wish to make it in the dark.

Around her, the forest was eerily silent, the usual evening chorus of birds and insects mute. It put her on edge, eyes flicking over the scraggly trees neighbouring the path. Their dense branches shifted with the wind, but otherwise there was no sign of movement.

She moved on.

Behind her the path wound down through the forest. The mountain on which their homestead perched stood alone amidst the Californian floodplains, looking out across their broad expanse. All around the rock were the lands of the Flores family – or at least the lands they managed. Once they had been theirs, but no longer.

Liz smiled as she approached the final bend in the track. The house was only a short thirty-minute walk up the moun-

tain, but she was still glad to see the end of it. It had been a long journey from San Francisco.

Around her the trees opened out, revealing the homestead sitting at the trail's end. Glancing around, Liz listened for the first shouts of welcome. Her family employed a dozen labourers on the property, and most were like family to her.

Silence.

A shiver went through Liz as she closed on the homestead. Her eyes flickered around the collection of buildings, searching for movement, for signs of life.

It was only then she saw the bodies.

They lay strewn across the homestead, torn and broken, their faces grey and dead. Blood splattered the walls nearby, streaked across the peeling paint. Her eyes swept over the bodies, lingering on their faces. There was Nancy, the old woman who had helped raise her, who had cooked meals while her mother helped in the fields. And there, Henry, the man her father thought of as a brother.

Standing amidst the carnage, Liz's eyes drifted up to the building she called home. Without thinking, she found herself moving towards it. Her movements were jerky, her breath coming as desperate sobs. Reaching the old wooden door, she pushed it open.

It swung inwards without resistance, revealing the wreckage within. Swallowing a scream, Liz staggered inside, eyes sweeping the shattered plaster walls, the torn-up floorboards. Dust and rubble lay strewn across the floor, mingling with the blood pooling at the end of the corridor.

Barely daring to breathe, Liz stepped inside the house. With cautious footsteps, she slid down the corridor, eyes fixed on the *blood. She winced at each soft tread of her boots, the sound impossibly loud in the silent house.*

The corner neared. In a sudden rush, Liz darted forward, eyes wide, desperate to see…

Liz screamed and threw up her arms, tearing herself from the nightmare. Her eyes snapped open, but absolute darkness stretched out around her and she screamed again, thrashing against the tangle of covers wrapped around her. The bed creaked as she rolled. The safety bar creaked as she slammed into it, then gave way. She found herself falling, plummeting through empty air, a final scream tearing from her throat.

Thud.

A bolt of agony lanced through her arms as she struck the concrete. The last tendrils of the dream fell away, plunging her back into reality – and the pain that went with it. She groaned, her throat burning as it pressed against the cold steel of her collar.

"What?" somewhere in the darkness, a voice shouted.

"Who's there?" someone else yelled.

"Liz?" She recognised Chris's voice.

Above her, his bunk rattled as he moved. Then hands were reaching for her, grasping her shoulder, pulling her up.

"Are you alright?" Chris's voice came again.

Half in shock, Liz couldn't manage more than a nod. Distantly, she was surprised at the tenderness in his words, his sudden concern. A second later, she realised he could not see her nod. Opening her mouth, she managed a croak. "Yes."

As sanity slowly returned, a wave of embarrassment swept through Liz. She closed her eyes, silently berating herself for her panic. It had been so long since she'd had the dream – months, maybe even a year. Why had it returned now, after all this time?

"What happened?" Sam's voice was heavy with sleep.

"Sorry," Liz murmured, heart still racing. "Was just a bad dream."

"Some bad dream," Ashley's hand settled on her shoulder. "Go back to bed, Sam. You need your beauty sleep."

A string of inaudible mumbling came from Sam's bed, quickly followed by a soft snore.

Arms shaking, Liz pulled herself up, helped by Chris on one side, Ashley on the other.

"It's okay," she murmured and then suppressed a groan.

Her throat was aflame, throbbing with each beat of her heart. She tried to swallow, but it only made the pain worse. The steel collar dug into her swollen throat. Gasping, she fought for breath.

"What's wrong?" Chris asked in the darkness, taking her weight beneath his shoulder.

"My throat," Liz gasped.

"Water." Somehow Chris understood. "Ashley, help me get her to the sink."

A sharp pain twisted through Liz's shin where she'd landed as she tried to take her weight. With a silent moan, she collapsed back against them. To her right, Ashley swore as the shift in weight sent her stumbling into the bed. Then she straightened, shifted her body beneath Liz's shoulder, and helped her the few steps to the sink.

Liz slumped to the ground as Ashley released her. The sound of water followed as Chris helped her to sit comfortably.

"Here," Ashley whispered. "Open your mouth, Liz. The water will help."

Liz obeyed as Ashley's hands fumbled at her face. She almost lost an eye before Ashley finally found her lips. Then cool water dripped into her mouth, trickling from the palm of the girl's hands. Swallowing slowly, Liz let out a long sigh as the cold spread down her throat.

They repeated the procedure three more times before Liz's breathing began to ease. At last she croaked for them to stop, and they settled back down together on Ashley's bed.

"How are you feeling now?" Ashley whispered.

In the other bed, Sam was still snoring. Listening in the darkness, Liz found herself jealous of the boy's ability to sleep through anything. She desperately needed the release of sleep, to escape the pain of her beaten body. But she knew it would not come now, not after the dream.

"I'm okay," she breathed. "You should go back to sleep."

A soft chuckle came from the girl. "My bed's a

little crowded now. It's okay, I think the lights will turn on soon."

Her words were met by a distant clang, followed by a low buzzing in the ceiling. Liz blinked as white light flooded the room, then raised an eyebrow at Ashley. She sat beside Liz, her yellow eyes ringed by shadow, the scarlet locks of her tangled with sleep. A smile tugged at her lips.

A groan came from the opposite bed as Sam rolled over and pulled the pillow over his head.

"God," Chris's voice came from her other side.

Liz turned to face him. "What?"

He blinked and shook his head. "Your neck, no wonder you couldn't breathe. It's a rather attractive shade of purple."

Liz lifted a hand and touched a finger to her throat, but flinched back as the muscles spasmed. She bit her lip, swallowing the pain. "I've had worse."

Chris shivered, but said nothing.

For the next few minutes they sat in silence, listening to the growing crescendo of Sam's snores. Finally, Ashley stood and moved across to his bed. Taking a hold of his blanket, she tore it away, exposing his half-naked body to the cold. His curses echoed from the walls as Ashley retreated to her bed, bringing Sam's cover with her.

Liz chuckled as Ashley spread the cover over them, trying to ignore the burning from her throat. "Thanks, I was getting cold," she grinned at the other girl.

"Hey!" Sam was sitting up now, blinking hard in

the fluorescent light. Lifting his pillow, he tossed it across the room. Chris caught it easily and placed it behind his head.

Liz smiled as a little of the weight lifted from her heart. Wriggling her backside, she snuggled in beneath the blanket, and basked in the warmth from either side of her. Together, they grinned as Sam found the shirt he'd discarded the night before and pulled it over his broad shoulders. Liz watched with a tinge of disappointment as he covered himself.

"Hey, my eyes are up here, ladies," Sam laughed.

Liz snorted. "Like I'd be interested in a city slugger like you, Sam."

Ashley giggled and Chris chuckled while Sam rolled his eyes. Then the clang of the outer door echoed down the corridor, plunging the room into silence. The smiles fell from their faces as they shared sad glances, the weight of yesterday's guilt returning.

"What happens next?" Chris murmured.

Sam's eyes flickered towards Ashley. "After we... survived, you two showed up," Sam replied with a shrug. "You know the rest."

Beside her, Ashley shifted on the bed. "Yesterday, on the training field, the doctors were talking," the girl spoke in a low voice. "I overheard a bit. They were talking about things moving ahead. So who knows what comes next."

The bed shifted again as Chris pulled himself up. A pang of sadness touched Liz as his warmth left her side. He moved to the bars and glanced down the corridor. "Well, whatever comes next, at least breakfast is on its way," his words were spoken with a false lightness, failing to hide the strain beneath, but Liz appreciated his attempt to brighten the gloomy discussion.

Sam groaned. "Don't suppose it's something other than that gruel they call oatmeal?"

"Sure, what's your order? I'll give them a shout." Chris laughed.

"I'll take some eggs with a side of bacon. Maybe some hash browns. Oh, and a burger. You got all that?"

"How about a television while you're at it, Chris?" Ashley put in.

Shaking his head, Chris returned to the bed and slid in beside Liz. "Ah, bacon. I can't even remember the last time we had that at home."

As his warmth touched Liz she found herself sliding closer, until her side pressed up against him. A tingle ran up her arm at the touch, and she held her breath, waiting for him to pull away. When he did not move, she smiled, only then recalling his words. Her grin spread. While the food on the ranch had not technically been theirs to eat, her family had made an art of pilfering extra supplies whenever they were available. Bacon had been just one of the many luxury food items she'd enjoyed.

"Oh, I don't know, back on the farm we had bacon and eggs for breakfast most days. It gets a little old."

She chuckled as the three of them turned to stare at her. Unfortunately, the laughter was too much for her throat, and she broke into a coughing fit. It was a few minutes before she found her voice again.

"Country secret," she croaked at last, and the others groaned.

The screeching wheels of the breakfast cart came to a sudden halt outside their cell. The guard banged his rifle against the bars while the other opened the grate through which they passed the food.

"Come and get it." The guard with the gun laughed. "Big day for you I hear."

Chris retrieved the four bowls of oatmeal, much to Sam's chagrin, and they sat down to their meal.

Afterwards the four of them sat back and waited, listening for the sound of the outer door. Closing her eyes, Liz did her best to ignore the agony that was her neck. Her good mood quickly fell away as the pain beat down on her. Silently, she cursed the doctors, the guards and their guns, even Joshua for his vicious attack.

"What do you think he meant?" Sam asked after an hour, addressing the room at large.

"Nothing good," Chris offered unhelpfully.

"Well, they need us alive for something," Ashley put in. She had joined Sam on the other bed now, surrendering her bed to Liz and Chris. "Whatever this place is, its top secret. My parents weren't the most connected of individuals in the government, but most things reached the rumour mill at some point. I don't think this place was ever mentioned. As far as the media are concerned, the children of traitors were…"

her voice trailed off, and Liz felt a pang of sadness for the girl.

Without speaking, Sam reached up and placed an arm around Ashley, drawing her into a hug. Watching them, Liz's sadness grew, rising from some lonely chasm inside her. The last two years had been long and hard, and more than once she had found herself craving the touch of another human being. Licking her lips, she glanced at Chris, then gave herself a silent shake. Drawing up her knees, she hugged them to her chest.

Movement came from beside her, but it was just Chris rearranging himself on the bed. He spoke into the uncomfortable silence. "Maybe it's the same with our families then. Maybe they've been taken some-place else," there was no mistaking the tremor of hope in his voice.

As the others nodded, Liz closed her eyes. The others might still cling to the hope their families were alive, but hers were gone.

"Wouldn't that be nice?" Sam replied with false cheer. "We can all have a reunion someday, share torture stories around the campfire—"

"Shut up, Sam." Ashley pushed him away and looked at Chris. "We can only hope, Chris. Although my sister…" she bowed her head, eyes shining. "She got in the way. They never gave her a chance."

Before any of them could respond, a loud clang echoed down the corridor.

The four of them exchanged a long glance.

"Showtime," Sam whispered.

CHAPTER 18

THE SOFT SCREECH of iron rollers carried down the corridor as the door to a cell slid open. Together, the four of them jumped from their beds and pressed themselves up against the bars. Head hard against the cold steel, Liz peered out into the corridor, straining to see what was happening. The faces of their fellow inmates appeared behind the bars of the other cells, eyes wide and staring.

At the very limits of her viewpoint, Liz could just make a group of doctors clustered around the cell at the end of the corridor, talking quietly amongst themselves. Beside them, guards were shouting at the occupants of the cell. They carried steel batons now, instead of the familiar rifles of the past few days.

As Liz watched, the guards disappeared into the cell. The raised voices of the prisoners carried to them, followed by the muffled thud of steel on flesh.

Retreating from the bars, Liz looked at the others. Sam and Chris stared back, their eyes wide, uncertainty written across their faces. Ashley only pursed her lips, her eyes roaming the cell.

Liz turned back to the bars as a girl's scream carried down the corridor. Looking along the rows of cells, she watched the doctors gathering around a steel trolley. One of the doctors was leaning over an open drawer on the side of the cart. Reaching inside, he drew out a packet of syringes. Vials of a clear liquid quickly followed, as he handed them out to the other doctors. Together, they turned and followed the guards into the cell. Another shriek echoed down the corridor, a boy's this time.

"What's going on?" Chris asked from behind her.

Liz glanced back at the others. "It's some sort of injection. They've got syringes and a trolley loaded with God knows what else."

As she finished speaking, a long, drawn out screeched erupted from the cell at the end of the corridor. Liz flinched, pressing her face hard against the bars, straining to see. It was the girl again. Distantly she remembered the faces of the two captives: a young girl with blonde hair, a boy with black dreadlocks.

The girl's scream slowly died away, but before it ceased the boy's voice joined in, carrying the awful notes of agony to the four of them in their little cell. Liz shuddered, fighting the urge to cover her ears. The shrieks rose and fell, twisting and cracking, almost inhuman in their anguish.

Turning, she saw the blood draining from the

other's faces, felt her own cheeks grow cold with an awful fear.

Slowly the screams died away, leaving only silence.

And the screech of trolley wheels on concrete as the doctors made their way to the next cell.

"What do we do?" Chris repeated his question from earlier.

"We fight," came Ashley's reply.

Liz turned and stared at the girl, heart thudding hard in her chest. "*What?*" from down the corridor came the rattle of another cell opening. "What about the collars—" she broke off as a cough tore at her throat.

Staggering past the others, she fumbled at the sink and turned the faucet. As she drank, Ashley continued to speak.

"Those batons, why do they need them?" her voice sounded calm, as though they were discussing the weather. "They haven't used them before now."

"It's like you said before," Sam mused. "They don't want us dead. They've been saving us for something. For *this.*"

"Really?" Chris snapped. He waved a hand. "Because I'm pretty sure they just killed those two."

"They're not using the collars," Liz croaked as she re-joined them. The realisation had come as she pressed her mouth to the faucet, making the collar dig into her neck. "No guns *or* collars."

Sam grinned and cracked his knuckles. "In that case, I agree with Ashley."

Liz leaned against the pole of her bunk bed,

drawing reassurance from its icy touch. She looked at the others, fear fluttering in her stomach. Sam looked more alive than she'd ever seen him, his eyes alight with a frightening rage. Chris stood beside him, tense and ready, one eye on the door to the cell.

And Ashley... just looked like Ashley – cool, calm, collected.

She pushed past the boys as another scream rattled the walls. As they took up station near the door, she crouched between the beds, and lifted a piece of railing which lay wedged against the wall. Liz blinked, realising it was the safety railing for her bed, the one that had given way and sent her crashing to the concrete.

Ashley moved across to Sam and offered him the bar. Teeth flashing, he took it and held it up to the light. The three parts of the rail formed a distorted U-shape, with two short piece of steel jutting from the longer centre piece.

"Work at the joints, see if you can break them apart."

As Sam set to work trying to separate the bars, Ashley moved to the front of the cell and resumed her watch. Liz joined her, and together they followed the doctors slow progress through the prison.

"They're done with us," Chris whispered behind them.

Outside the screams continued, at times slowly fading, only to resume as the doctors reached the next cell.

"No," Ashley whispered. Her eyes took on a

haunted look. "I think they're only just getting started."

"Here." Liz turned and Sam offered her one of the smaller bars. He grinned. "Just pretend they're city sluggers like me."

Liz smiled back. Silently she reached out and squeezed his arm. He nodded and moved across to Ashley and Chris, offering them the other two bars. Ashley took one, but Chris shook his head. His eyes did not leave the corridor, but he spoke from the side of his mouth.

"I'd prefer to keep my hands free, thanks."

Outside, the doctors had reached the cell directly across from them. Its only occupant stood at the bars, watching as the doctors drew to a halt. His eyes were bloodshot and tears streamed down his face.

"Please, I never did anything wrong," his voice was feeble, barely a whisper.

He retreated into his cell as the guards slid the door open. Before he could so much as raise his fists they were on him, batons flashing in the fluorescent lights. A few seconds later they had him pinned to the bed. Without preamble, the doctors entered the cell. As the guards held the boy down, one doctor pulled down his pants, while another prepared the needle. The injection was given, then the doctors and guards retreated from the cell, slamming the door closed behind them.

Liz flinched as the boy screamed and began to writhe. Then the guards moved between them and the other cell, and there was no more time to consider their neighbour's plight.

Gripping the bars of their cell tight in her hands, Liz watched as the guards gathered near the door. The pain in her throat had strangely faded away, leaving only a dull ache. Blood pounded in her ears as she tensed, readying herself.

"Stand back, drop those," one of the guards ordered, eying their makeshift batons.

When they didn't move, he turned to look at the doctors.

"What are you waiting for?" Doctor Radly's voice carried into the cell. "Get in there and take those off them. You know we can't use the collars. We can't have any interference with their nervous system."

The guard nodded and reached out to unlock the door. The others gathered behind him, seven in total, their batons held ready.

A strange calm settled over Liz as the door slid open, the terror of the past few days falling away. Whatever Ashley thought, this was it. This was their only chance. If they failed, she knew in her heart they would be lost.

As the first of the guards moved into the cell, movement came from beside her. She turned in time to see Chris lunge forward. The guard grinned and raised his baton, but Chris was faster still. Leaping lightly from the concrete floor, he twisted in the air to avoid the man's blow, and drove a kick into the side of the guard's head.

Liz gaped as the man's eyes rolled up in his skull and he collapsed to the ground

Chris landed lightly in the doorway and retreated back to re-join them.

"Six to go," he grinned, his smile infectious.

Shaking her head, Liz gripped the metal bar tighter and tried to hide her shock.

Outside, the remaining guards grabbed their fallen comrade by the feet and dragged his unconscious body out into the corridor. One of the doctors crouched beside him and placed a stethoscope to his chest. Radly glanced down at the man, then back at the guards. Each of them dwarfed even Sam's large frame, but still they stood hesitating in the hallway. The fate of their comrade had given them pause.

"Well?" he snapped. "What are we paying you for? Get in there!"

The guards shared a glance, then approached together. Pushing the sliding door wide open, they entered as a group this time. They paused for a second in the entrance-way, hefting their batons, then came forward in a sudden rush.

Liz tensed as the first guard came for her, his steel baton flashing for her face. Ducking back, the hackles on her neck tingled as it swept over her head. Then she lifted her own weapon and drove it into the man's midriff.

The blow caught him as he was moving forward, and his own weight drove the air from his lungs. As he staggered to a halt, Liz lifted her bar to strike him again, then threw herself to the side as another guard swung at her. Steel rang out as the baton left a dent in the bunk bed behind her.

Recovering, she turned and found the first guard already straightening. Now the two of them bore down on her, forcing her away from the others.

Liz gripped her makeshift weapon tight, knowing she was hopelessly outmatched. Snarling, she threw herself forward anyway. They grinned, raised their batons. Then a body stumbled backwards into them, sending them stumbling forward. Seeing her chance, Liz swung her pole into the face of the nearest guard.

As the man staggered sideways, she leapt for the gap he'd left, eager to re-join the others. But as she moved, the other recovered and stepped in to block her, baton already in motion. The blow caught her in the stomach, knocking the breath from her lungs and sending her staggering backwards into the wall.

Groaning, she tried to straighten, but a fist caught her in the side of the face. Her feet crumpled beneath the force of the blow, and she slid sideways into the crook between the wall and the bunk. Coughing up blood, she tried to regain her feet, but a heavy boot crashed into her back, pinning her to the ground.

Head ringing, Liz twisted on the ground, desperate for a glimpse of the others. But the fight was already over, the guards' weight and numbers making short work of the four prisoners in the narrow confines of the cell. Sam lay immobilised on his own bed, a guard's knee pressed between his shoulder blades. Ashley was similarly restrained on the floor nearby, while Chris still stood, his arms held by a man on either side of him. The last guard was just getting to his feet, a nasty bruise on his forehead.

"About time," Radly's sarcastic voice came from somewhere out of view. "Would you like something easier next time. Maybe some toddlers?"

The guards were silent as the doctors filed in, carrying their assortment of vials and syringes. As the doctors prepared themselves, Radly looked around the room. His eyes settled on Liz. "Get her up."

Tears stung Liz's eyes as a rough hand grasped a handful of her hair and pulled. Screaming, she drove a fist into the man's side, but the blow hardly seemed to faze him. A tearing pain came from her scalp as he pulled again. Kicking and screaming, Liz found herself hauled to her feet.

"This one's feisty," the guard commented as he tossed her onto Ashley's bed.

Before Liz could free herself, the weight of the guard landed on her back. An awful helplessness welled in her as she tried and failed to shift his weight. Pain lanced from her scalp again as the guard yanked her head back, forcing her to look at them.

"Stay still," the guard growled in her ear.

"Please don't do this," Ashley pleaded from the floor.

The thud of a boot striking flesh silenced her desperate words. A low groan followed. Liz twisted again, trying to get a glimpse of her friend, but the white coat of a doctor moved to block her view. Looking up, she saw Doctor Radly staring down at her.

"Enough," Radly's tone brooked no argument.

Unlike Halt, Radly did not appear to take any joy in their pain. Rather, he didn't seem to care about their comfort one way or another. He moved around the cell with a cold efficiency, retrieving the stoppered vial from the hands of another doctor. Lifting a nasty looking syringe, he eyed the thick needle for a second before driving it through the vial's rubber stopper. Then he drew back the plunger, watching as the liquid disappeared into the syringe.

"Doctor Faulks," Radly addressed someone standing just outside of Liz's view. "This is the PERV-A strain?"

"Yes," a woman's reply came quickly. "We've already finished with the B strain. The rest are marked down for PERV-A."

Nodding, Radly turned back to Liz. "Hold her," Liz shuddered as the guard shifted, taking a firmer hold of her shoulders.

From the corner of her eye, she watched Radly approach, his gloved hands holding the syringe in a gentle grip. Then he disappeared from her line of vision. Seconds later firm hands tugged at her pants, and a cold breeze blew across her backside. She tensed, pushing back against her assailant's relentless strength.

A sigh came from behind her. "This will go easier for you if you relax, Ms Flores."

Hearing her last name sent a bolt of shock through Liz. For a second she hesitated, then bit off a string a profanity that would have made her father blush.

Another sigh, then a cold cloth pressed against her butt-cheek. A shiver raced up her spine, more shock from the violation than from the cold. A low, guttural growl built in her throat, and the guard's knee pressed harder into the small of her back. But she no longer cared. A desperate horror was growing within her, an awful fear, a need to break free.

She screamed again, writhing and bucking beneath the guard, straining to shift his weight.

A sudden pinch came from her naked backside, followed by a cool pressure that spread quickly across her cheek. It was gentle at first, a cold numbness that tingled as it went. But it quickly warmed, like a fire gathering heat, until her muscles were aflame from its touch. The tingle raced outwards, spreading the numbing sensation to her legs and arms.

Liz gasped, fighting back against the pain, desperate to fend it off. She gritted her teeth, tensing against its relentless spread. The pressure on her back vanished as the guard released her, but by then she barely noticed. Her attention was elsewhere, her focus fixed on the waves of sensation rippling through her body.

Then as though a switch had been flicked, the muscles down the length of her back locked in a sudden cramp. Pain unlike any she'd experienced closed around her, walling her off from the world, trapping her in the iron arms of its cage. Her eyes snapped open, but all she saw were stars, whirling through her vision, blinding in their brilliance. In the distance she heard a scream, a girl's voice tearing at the blackness of her mind, but she could do nothing to help her now.

Agony engulfed her body, her mind, her very soul.

CHAPTER 19

COLD.

The thought filtered through the thick sludge of Chris's mind, parting the darkness like a curtain. Then it was all around him, wrapping his body in an icy blanket, turning his breath to ragged gasps. A shiver caught him, rippling down his body, throwing off the last dredges of sleep.

Frozen air burned his nostrils as he inhaled, bringing with it the familiar tang of bleach. But there was more to the scent now, an underlying stench of rot and decay that made his stomach swirl. Opening his mouth, he tasted the metallic reek of blood and vomit on the air.

Sound quickly followed the return of his taste and smell. His ears tingled, catching the murmur of a breath, the creak of metal joints moving beneath restless bodies, the hiss of an air conditioner. From somewhere in the room came the rattle of chains, the familiar whine of the overhead lights.

I'm alive, the words whispered in Chris's mind, though he couldn't quite recall why that surprised him.

Keeping his eyes closed, Chris sucked in another breath, struggling to restore the shattered pieces of his consciousness. Dimly he remembered the fire burning up his spine, spreading to his chest, filling his lungs. But there was no pain now, only the dull ache of his muscles, as though they had lain unused for countless days.

How long? His brow creased.

How long had he lain there, unconscious, in the clutches of whatever drug the doctors had given him?

Sounds echoed from all around him, growing louder as he lay there, echoing as though from a wide expanse. Chains rattled as he moved his arms, and he felt the cold touch of steel restraining his wrists. Without opening his eyes, he realised he had been handcuffed to the bed.

Apparently they were still taking no chances with their patients.

Memories drifted through the darkness of his thoughts, rising as though from a fog. Images of the fight flashed by, the crack as Sam fell to a baton, the thud of Ashley hitting the floor. He had not seen what happened to Liz, not until the guards had overwhelmed him, and he'd found her curled up in the corner.

Helpless, he had watched as Liz was lifted onto the bed and injected. Her screams had been instant and horrifying, so deafening even the guards had retreated from her. Her agony tore at his soul, begged for him to save her from the monsters. But he had been powerless against the raw strength of the men on either side of him.

His heart beat harder as thoughts of the girl rose in his mind. A sense of urgency took him, and he shifted his arms, testing the movement allowed by the handcuffs. The links rattled as he ran a hand along the chain, and found where the handcuffs attached to a guard rail running horizontally along the side of his bed.

Other sounds came to him now: the beeping of a nearby machine, the whir of a pump, the hiss of air escaping tubes. Listening, he heard the steady beeps accelerating, matching the racing of his heart.

Somewhere in the room, a door banged. Chris froze, his fingers still clenched around the metal bar. The soft tread of footsteps moved through the room, followed by voices.

"Has the danger passed?" Halt's voice came from Chris's right.

"We think so." He recognised Fallow, though her voice was strained, exhausted. "It was a close thing though. I told you it wasn't ready."

"Perhaps," Halt replied. "But we expected losses. Despite our best efforts, some of the candidates were simply too weak to withstand the morphological alterations."

"We lost forty percent!" Chris winced as Fallow's voice cracked. He heard a long inhalation of breath, before she continued in a calmer voice. "I expected mortality to be less than fifteen. As it is, we barely have a viable population... If we'd had more time..."

"More time?" Halt laughed. "That is the cry of a coward, Fallow! More time, more money, always more *something!*" he took a breath. "As Archimedes once said: 'Give me a lever and a place to stand, and I will move the earth.' But we only have the time and resources the government has provided us with. And our time is up."

"The *government* will not be satisfied with a forty percent mortality rate, Halt," Fallow growled.

"No," came the head doctor's swift reply. "But if the survivors show promise, you will have won the time you need to find perfection, Fallow."

Silence followed. Slowly their footsteps came closer. Listening to the beep of the machine beside him, Chris held his breath, struggling to slow his racing heart.

"And have we succeeded, Fallow?" Halt's voice was eager.

It was a while before the woman replied. "The results are mixed. Tissue samples taken over the last few weeks have shown steady integration between the host chromosomes and the viral DNA. Candidates who received the PERV-B strain have advanced more rapidly than PERV-A, and now show complete integration. However, we are yet to determine whether the altered genomes are expressing correctly."

"Excellent," there was unmasked glee in Halt's voice. "When do you expect them to be ready to test genome expression?"

"We've taken them off the immunosuppressants, and so far, they have shown no adverse reactions. We expect them to begin waking from their comas over the next few days. Once they're conscious, we can begin testing their basic motor skills and cognitive function, to determine whether the virus had any degenerative effects..." Fallow trailed off as Halt snorted.

"We don't have time to waste on your procedures, Fallow. We need *results*."

"I don't see how—" Fallow began.

"Don't give me that, Fallow," Halt snapped. "You know very well there is no need for those tests. As far as the directors are concerned, we have either succeeded or failed. There is only one test the candidates need to pass to show that."

There was a long pause before Fallow replied. "Halt..." her voice was entreating now. "That's simply not possible. They've been unconscious for weeks. The recovery time alone... They're in no condition—"

"If the experiment succeeded, recovery time should not be an issue," Halt's voice sounded like he was just a few feet away. "Look, this one appears to be conscious."

On the bed, a tingle raced up Chris's spine. Silently he held his breath, fighting the instinct to leap from the bed and flee. His arms prickled as goose bumps spread along his skin.

"You're right," Fallow's murmur seemed to come

from directly overhead. "Her heartbeat has recovered to normal levels.

A girl's cry tore the air, followed by the angry rattle of chains. Chris cracked his eye open a fraction, desperate to see what was happening. Pain shot through his skull as white light streamed between his eyelids, momentary blinding him. Then the light faded and the room clicked into sudden focus. Beyond the rails of his bed, rows of beds stretched out across a wide room, each occupied by an unconscious patient dressed in green scrubs. A tangle of tubes and wires wrapped around each body like a spider web spun around a fly. From the brief glimpse he caught, Chris guessed there were some thirty beds, though many were empty.

The girl Halt and Fallow were discussing was sitting up in the hospital bed directly across from Chris. Her back was turned to him, and she had both arms chained to the bed. Curly black hair tumbled down the back of her scrubs, and with a shiver of recognition, Chris realised it was Liz.

She's alive!

Chris struggled to muffle his sharp intake of breath. Beside him, the beep of the machine started to race. Silently he clenched the sidebar of his bed until his palms hurt. Through the shadows of his eyelashes, he watched Halt move to stand over Liz.

"Incredible." Halt was studying the machine beside Liz's bed. Lines and numbers flashed across the screen, he guessed providing readings from the long tubes and wire that covered Liz. "Look at her vitals."

Fallow stood in silence beside him, shadows ringing her eyes, her lips pursed tight.

Halt shook his head and looked at her. "I would say she is fully recovered, wouldn't you, Doctor Fallow."

Reluctantly Fallow nodded, a look of resignation coming over her face.

"Excellent, then I see no reason to delay. Get her ready."

Blood pounded in Chris's head as a sudden rage swept through him. He didn't know what Halt had planned for Liz, what fresh horror he had in store, but he refused to lie quietly while she faced it alone. Whatever happened, they were still in this together. For all he knew, Sam and Ashley might already be gone, but Liz still lived. He would not lose her now.

"Leave her alone," he growled, sitting up in the bed.

On the other bed, Liz turned towards him, her eyes widening with shock. Behind her, Fallow's face seemed to crumple, while a grin spread slowly across Halt's face. In that instant, Chris felt a pit open in his stomach; a sudden realisation he had made a terrible mistake.

Still, it was worth it to see the relief sweep across Liz's face.

"Excellent." Halt clapped his hands. "Bring him too. It may even the odds."

CHAPTER 20

Liz shivered as Fallow unlocked the cuffs around her wrists. Blinking, she stared at the woman's face. Her features faded in and out of focus, and a bolt of nausea swept through her stomach. She wrapped a hand around the sidebar to steady herself and blinked again.

"Are you okay?" Liz flinched as a hand touched her shoulder.

"*Don't!*" she growled, leaning back.

Closing her eyes, Liz willed her stomach to settle, then opened them again. To her relief, the features of Fallow's face finally snapped into place. She blinked again, surprised to see the dark rings beneath the woman's eyes, the patchwork of tiny cracks across the skin of her cheeks, the thin red capillaries threading her eyes. Her head swam; she had never noticed such detail in someone's face before.

"I'm sorry." Liz's ears twitched at the sound, before a harsh shriek cut through the words.

She recoiled and slapped her hands over her ears. Distantly she heard the doctor's voice over the ringing. A hand reached for her, but she twisted, falling sideways on the bed. Fallow paused, staring down at her, and then retreated a step.

Slowly the ringing died away, and Liz finally removed her hands from her ears.

"I'm sorry," Fallow's voice was a whisper now, but she heard it with perfect clarity, "How do you feel?"

Grating her teeth, Liz shook her head and looked across at Chris. As their eyes met her heart gave a lurch, and she felt again the relief that had swept through her when he'd sat up.

He's alive!

Despite the apparent odds against them, somehow the two of them had survived whatever demented experiment the doctors had performed on them. Beside her, Fallow had busied herself removing the various tubes and wires that had been hooked up to the machine. Swallowing the surge of hate clogging her throat, Liz faced her.

"Why are you doing this?" Liz could not keep the resignation from her voice.

Fallow sighed, her eyes closing a moment before she looked at Liz. "You'll find out soon enough, Elizabeth."

Liz stared at the grief shining from Fallow's eyes. Despite herself, Liz felt pity for the woman. Even so, the doctor's words triggered a sense of foreboding within her, and she pressed on, desperate to exploit the woman's weakness.

"You don't have to do this," she whispered. "Halt's gone. You could let us go, unlock these collars."

A faint smile twitched at Fallow's lips. "A tempting proposition," she shook her head. "They'd kill you both before you even reached the front door. Then they would come for me." Her amber eyes locked on Liz. She stared back in silent appeal. But Fallow only smiled and continued on with false humour. "Besides, you are the culmination of my life's work."

"What about *our* lives?" Chris's snarl came from behind Liz. "What right—"

He broke off as Fallow raised a hand. She shook her head again, her smile fading. "You know the law, Christopher. Your mother was found guilty of treason. In due time, she will answer for those crimes. As her son, you would have faced the same fate."

Even to Liz, Fallow's words sounded hollow, spoken like they left a bad taste in her mouth. Even so, after that the woman ignored their pleas. Moving across to Chris, she removed the cuffs and wires. Within a few minutes she had them on their feet and staggering around the room like senior citizens.

Liz's legs trembled with each step, refusing to obey the simplest instructions. A dull ache was quickly spreading up her hamstrings, and several times she had to grab at neighbouring beds to steady herself. Chris was no better; managing to knock over a series of machines within two steps of leaving his bed, after which he promptly crashed to the linoleum floor.

From the corner of her eyes, Liz caught movement from several of the beds, but the doctor was too preoccupied with Chris to notice. Steadying herself, she took a moment to search the room for Ashley and Sam. But as the fluorescent light caught in her eyes she found their focus shifting again, and the room began to blur. By the time her vision cleared, Fallow was already shepherding them towards the doorway.

Outside, Liz's legs finally began to obey, though they remained stiff and sore. Chris was steadily improving too, but he still needed her shoulder to keep moving down the narrow corridor. Two guards stood on either side of the door to the room, but they made no move to follow them. Fallow kept pace several feet behind them though, no doubt ready to use the collars should they place a foot out of line.

Step by faltering step, they made their way through the facility, obeying Fallow's direction whenever they came to an intersection of corridors. After a few turns, Chris could walk unaided, though it was a while before he managed more than a slow stumble. Fortunately for him, the doctor did not seem to be in any hurry.

But despite their slow pace, the journey could not last forever, and far too little time had passed before they found themselves outside a familiar white door. Liz shivered as she recognised it, memories of her fight with Joshua spiralling through her mind.

She turned as Fallow spoke from behind them. "Go in."

Wordlessly, Liz shook her head. Dread wrapped around her stomach as she reached out and took

Chris's hand. Together they faced the doctor, standing straight now, the strength slowly returning to their limbs.

"We won't," Liz drew herself up and stepped towards Fallow. "I won't."

Fallow retreated a step. She lifted her arm, the watch on her wrist flashing in warning. "Won't what?" Fallow asked.

"I won't fight her." Chris coughed, stepping up beside Liz. "I'd rather die."

Fallow's shoulders slumped and she gave a little shake of her head. "That's not... no," she gestured with a hand. "Just go."

Liz and Chris shared a glance, still hesitating. Despite Fallow's strange reassurance, fear gnawed at Liz's stomach; a dread she could not shake. The last time she had entered this room, an innocent boy had lost his life. And she had almost lost her own. Her hand drifted to her throat, but there was no pain now, only the cold reminder of the collar nestled beneath her chin.

How long were we asleep?

"Don't make me use the collars." Fallow lifted her finger to her watch.

They went.

As the door clicked shut behind her, Liz found herself standing again in the padded room, blinking in the brilliant light. An awful smell wafted through the air, a sickly sweet that caught in her throat. As her vision cleared, and the room came into focus, she realised with a sharp breath they were not alone.

A boy stood in the centre of the room. He wore the same plain orange jumpsuit they had sported in the cells, though she had never seen him there. His head was bowed, and his breath came in ragged gasps, his shoulders trembling with each violent exhalation. He held his hands clenched at his side, and though his eyes were open, he did not seem to have noticed them. Black hair dangled in front of his face, obscuring the rest of his features.

Liz edged towards him, her heart beating hard in her chest. Behind her, Chris gasped, and she felt his hand on her shoulder. But she twisted free, her panic rising. Gripped by a desperate need to see, to know for sure, she slid closer.

Leaning down, she peered into the boy's eyes.

Hard grey eyes stared back, their surface glazed with sleep, unseeing.

But as she stared, they blinked, the life behind them stirring.

And Liz screamed.

CHAPTER 21

CHRIS RECOGNISED it the instant they stepped into the room. Though outwardly it looked no different than any other boy, a strangeness hung about his hunched figure. The stench of him was strong in the room, a sickly sweetness that clung to the air.

He didn't need to see the grey eyes to know what it was.

Chead.

He had tried to stop Liz as she stepped towards it, but she only shook herself free and crept closer. Clenching his fists, he tested his strength, feeling it quickly returning. Silently, he watched as Liz bent to peer into the boy's face.

Then she was staggering backwards, her screams reverberating around the room. The *Chead's* features contorted, the ripple of awakening sweeping across its face, and then Chris was retreating too, fumbling at the door, shouting for help, knowing it would not come.

Beside him, Liz screamed again and staggered sideways. His hand flashed out, catching her by her scrubs, dragging her back to him as she began to thrash. Her panic swept over him, waking him from his stupor, and he shoved her behind him.

When he looked up, he caught the iron-grey eyes of the *Chead* staring at him. A smile spread across its face, and sent pure terror screaming through every fibre of his being. Another shriek came from behind him as Liz pounded on the padded door.

Taking a breath, Chris took a step towards the *Chead*, an eerie calm coming over him. He placed himself squarely between Liz and the creature, ignoring the urge to turn and shake her, to pull the girl back from the depths of her terror. But her words were still fresh in his mind, and he heard again the agony in her voice as she told him of her parents' death.

He could not blame her for panicking.

Staring into the eyes of the *Chead*, Chris searched for a sign of life, for a hint of the human it had once been.

In the centre of the room, the *Chead* raised an eyebrow. "Welcome," the word sounded strange, almost metallic, as though speech did not come easily to it.

For a second all Chris could do was stand and gape. He blinked, moving his mouth, struggling to find the words. "Wha– what?" he finally managed.

Grey eyes flickered from Chris to Liz. Then with deliberate slowness, the *Chead* turned and began to pace. It walked towards the mirror first, pausing as the boy's image rose up before it, a snarl twisting its lips. Then is spun, moving back past Chris and Liz until it reached the far wall, where it turned to make another pass. Metal shone around its neck, and for the first time Chris realised it wore a collar around its neck.

"What. Am. I?" The creature ground out the words. It paused and looked straight at Chris. "You already know that…"

Chris did not reply. His mind was still reeling, struggling to comprehend one irresolvable fact: it spoke. The *Chead* could speak – not just that, it could understand him. No newspaper, no television channel had ever mentioned a *Chead* speaking, never mind being self-aware. As far as the public were concerned, the *Chead* were monsters – uncontrollable, terrible, killing machines.

They did not think.

They did not speak.

"How?" Chris croaked.

By the door, he could sense Liz slowly regaining her composure. The thuds on the door had ceased, her screams dying to soft gasps. Movement came from beside him and on trembling legs Liz re-joined him. Out of the corner of his eye he watched a shiver run through her and reached out an arm. Their hands touched, their fingers entwining. He gave her hand a quick squeeze and turned back to the *Chead*.

It had stopped its pacing and stood again in the centre of the room, its grey eyes watching them. Its nostrils flared as it inhaled.

"You… smell different," it grated, then. "How do I speak?" it finished Chris's question.

Chris nodded his confirmation.

A smile spread across the *Chead's* face. "I learnt," it nodded, its head leaning to the side. "I remembered…"

A tremor ran through Liz's hand, but when he looked at the girl her eyes remained fixed straight ahead, her lips pressed tight together.

The *Chead's* head twisted strangely again, as though in curiosity. "You are different," it said again, its smile spreading, though there was no humour in the grey eyes. "Like me."

Chris's stomach clenched at its words.

What does it mean?

"What did you mean, you remembered?" Liz interrupted his thoughts.

The *Chead's* eyes flickered in her direction. "I remembered. Who I was… Before…" the boy shrugged.

Liz's fingers tightened around Chris's hand. He waited for her to speak, but she had fallen silent again.

"What do you mean? That we're like you?" Chris croaked.

An awful laughter crackled up from the thing's throat. "They succeeded, these jailers of ours," the boy's face twisted horribly, until it seemed some demon now possessed the boy. Speech seemed to come easier to it now. "But I wonder, is it enough?"

It stepped towards them then, the grin fading.

As one, Chris and Liz retreated across the padded floor, until their backs pressed against the door.

Chris raised his hands in surrender. "Please, wait, you don't have to do this."

The *Chead* paused, the hard glint in its eyes wavering. Then it shook its head. "But I do. It is my nature, isn't it?" It took another step, its eyes flickering to the one-way glass. "Besides, it's what *they* want."

Snarling, the *Chead* leapt towards them.

Without pausing to think, Chris pushed Liz away from him and stepped up to meet the creature's charge. From the corner of his eye he saw Liz stagger sideways, then the *Chead* was on him, its fist flashing for his chest. Acting on instinct, he threw up an arm, and the blow glanced from his forearm.

Chris gasped as pain jolted through his arm. Then the weight of the creature crashed into him, flinging him back into the wall. Before he could recover, the *Chead* had him by the shoulders. His stomach twisted as the long arms lifted him. Panic took him, and he kicked out with a foot, sending a desperate blow into the boy's head.

To his surprise, the *Chead* reeled back from the blow. A savage growl came from its throat as it tossed him aside. Chris bent his head and braced as the ground raced towards him. With a thud he struck, then he was rolling forward, spinning to come to his feet in one fluid movement. Straightening, he turned to face the *Chead*.

The creature stared back, the grey eyes watching

him like a predator stalking its prey. Slowly it lifted an arm and wiped a trickle of blood from its lip.

His gaze flickered as he caught sight of Liz. She moved to join him, eyes flashing. "Don't do that again," she growled.

Nodding, Chris turned his attention back to the *Chead*. It seemed hesitant now. Chris was glad for its caution. On the television, he had watched *Chead* tear policemen apart, seen throats torn out and skulls shattered by a single blow. Tasers did little to slow them, and bullets only seemed to anger them unless they struck something vital.

Unarmed and trapped in the tiny room, Chris did not like their odds.

Yet somehow his blow had rattled it.

Pushing down his fear, Chris edged away from Liz. Whatever their chances, they had to try. Between them, they at least outnumbered the *Chead* two to one. They had to make the most of that advantage.

The *Chead* snarled as he moved, its head turning to follow him. From the corner of his eyes, Chris watched Liz slide sideways in the opposite direction. The *Chead* ignored her though, clearly seeing Chris as the greater threat.

Chris just hoped Liz had the strength to prove it wrong.

The *Chead's* grin returned as Chris came to a stop. A low rumble quivered in its chest. It stepped towards him, legs tensing to spring. In reply, Chris raised his fists. He slid one leg back and twisted sideways, placing himself in a defensive stance. Flashing a smile he did not feel, he gestured the creature forward.

His impudence ignited a flash of anger in the *Chead's* eyes. Adrenaline pounded in Chris's veins as it stepped in close, washing away his fear. He reacted without thought, years of training taking over. One hand swept up to deflect the blow sweeping for his face. His arm shook as the force of the blow sent him reeling, but stepping back he kept his balance, his eyes already watching for the next attack.

Another fist flashed towards him and he ducked. As he moved, his surprise grew. He had seen a blow from a *Chead* shatter a man's arm with a single blow. By all rights, his arm should have been crushed. Yet somehow he was holding his own.

The *Chead* had realised this too, and snarling it hurled itself at Chris with renewed fury. A fist flashed beneath his guard and smashed into his stomach. The breath hissed between Chris's teeth as his lungs emptied. He squeezed a half-choked groan from his chest as the *Chead* stepped in close.

Then with a shriek, Liz leapt into the fray. Bent in two and gasping, Chris caught a glimpse of her tangled hair and flashing blue eyes as she drove her foot down into the back of the *Chead's* knee.

Screaming, it collapsed beneath the blow.

THE SECOND LIZ saw the stony grey eyes of the *Chead*, the memories had come flooding back. For a second she had found herself back in her parent's house, in the home she had been raised in. Once it had been a safe place, a sanctuary amidst the harsh world outside.

Now though, in her memories a perpetual shadow hung over its wooden hallways, sucking out the light, the life it had once born.

In her mind, she saw again the rubble-strewn corridor, the broken floor boards and pooling blood. She saw herself turn the corner, saw the body lying in the corridor, strangely whole, where those outside had lain in pieces.

And her mother, standing over the body, her grey eyes staring.

With a scream, Liz tore herself from the memory, returning herself to the present, to the room and Chris.

And the *Chead*.

Still reeling, caught in the clutches of remembered horror, she had barely heard the conversation between Chris and the *Chead*, the revelations it offered. She already knew the truth, that some semblance of their former lives clung to the creatures.

Why else had she been spared?

She had only truly woken when Chris pushed her from the path of *Chead's* charge. Angry flames had lit her stomach, waking her from the fear, restoring her to life.

Now as she edged sideways around the *Chead*, she let that anger grow, fed it with every injustice she had ever suffered. It was her only weapon now, her only strength against the sheer ferocity of the creature standing between them. Opposite her, Chris faced the creature, drawing it away, until its back was turned to her. But before she could strike, the *Chead* leapt for Chris.

Fear chilled her stomach as blows crashed against flesh. But to her surprise, Chris did not go down. Edging closer, she saw him deflect another blow, his arms moving faster than thought, the crack of fists connecting with bone ringing from the walls.

Liz stared, mouth wide with disbelief. What she was watching was not possible. Chris was keeping pace with the violent speed of the *Chead*, matching it blow for blow, punch for punch. Her eyes could barely keep up with their frenzied movements. The air itself seemed to shake with the strength of each blow, and still Chris stood, holding his own.

What have they done to us?

Her skin tingled as the question whispered in her mind. But there was no time to contemplate the thought, no time to consider its implications. Instead, she gathered herself and slid closer, searching for an opening.

Then a blow slid beneath Chris's guard. It slammed into his stomach and drove him to his knees. The colour fled his face as the *Chead* stepped in, raising a fist to deliver the final blow.

Seeing her chance, Liz sprang forward and drove the heel of her foot into the back of the *Chead's* knee. Idly she hoped whatever changes had been wrought on the *Chead* had not removed the cluster of nerve endings located behind the kneecap.

The bloodcurdling shriek that issued from the boy's throat answered her question. The *Chead's* legs crumbled beneath the force of the blow, sending it crashing to the ground. Clenching her teeth, Liz stepped up behind it as Chris rolled away.

She swung a kick at its head. But the *Chead* was already recovering, and quick as a cobra it twisted. Hands flashed out and caught her by the leg. Before she could free herself, it stood, grey eyes glittering. A low growl came from its throat as it lifted her. Gasping, she fought to break its hold, but its hands were like iron. Knowing it was useless, Liz lashed out with a fist, and caught it on the cheek.

A shock ran up her arm as the blow connected. The fingers around her leg loosened, and suddenly she was falling. Twisting, she landed awkwardly and looked up to see the *Chead* stumbling backwards, one hand raised to its cheek. With a growl, it straightened, and the grey eyes swept down to find her on the floor.

Liz felt her courage crumble as her eyes caught in its iron gaze. All semblance of its humanity had fled, melting in the red-hot flames of its rage. Hardly daring to breathe, she backed towards Chris, all thoughts of strategy falling away.

Snarling, it stepped after her.

"Now you've done it," Chris panted, his hand reaching for hers.

She clenched her hand around his, drawing strength from his presence, and then released him. Together they watched the *Chead* approach.

With a roar, it leapt.

Chris sprang forward, screaming his defiance. Stepping in front of Liz, he deflected the first swing of the creature's fist. But this time the force of the blow sent him reeling, and Liz had to step aside to avoid him. Then the *Chead* was on them, fists flying, lips drawn back in a snarl, its half-mad screams echoing from the mirrored glass.

A fist caught Liz in the cheek, staggering her, then the *Chead's* shoulder crashed into her chest. The breath rushed from her lungs as she hurtled backwards into the wall. Her head whipped back and struck the padding. Despite the soft surface, her vision spun from the blow. With a groan, she slid down the wall, struggling to catch her winded breath.

Across the room, Chris fought on. But he was no longer a match for the *Chead's* strength. And it was faster now, its speed and ferocity far beyond human capabilities. With contempt it knocked aside his blows. A fist crashed into his face, sending him stumbling backwards, but he refused to yield. Straightening, he launched himself back into the fray.

Desperate to aid him, Liz struggled back to her feet.

A shout drew her attention back to the fight. The *Chead* had caught Chris's fist in one hand. As she watched Chris screamed again, though this time neither of them had moved. An awful *crack* came from Chris's fist as he sank to his knees. The colour fled his face and he gave an awful groan. One handed, he struggled to regain his feet, until the *Chead's* free hand smashed into the side of his head. Chris slumped to the side then, his breathing ragged, one hand still caught in the creature's grip.

Silently, Liz pulled herself up. The *Chead's* back was turned to her, its attention focused on tearing Chris limb from limb. She flinched as another blow thudded into Chris's head. This time he made no effort to avoid the blow. A low gurgle came from his throat as the *Chead* lifted its arm, dragging him back to his feet.

Liz moved quickly, knowing she only had seconds to act. The soft floor made no noise beneath her bare feet. Without pausing to think, Liz hurled herself at the creature's back. This time she aimed high, sweeping her forearm over its shoulder. Before it could react, she pulled her arm tight against its throat and leaned back. Her feet caught the ground, giving her purchase, and she pulled harder, bending it backwards, dragging it off balance.

The *Chead* gave a strangled cry. Releasing Chris, it turned its attention on Liz. Knowing she could not match its strength or weight, Liz allowed herself to fall backwards, taking the *Chead* with her. The thud as its weight landed on her drove the breath from her lungs, but still she held on, forearm tight across its throat.

Sensing its plight, the *Chead* thrashed against her. Its legs kicked out, catching Liz in the shins. Pain lanced from her leg as something went *crack*, but no force on earth would make her let go now.

Not even death.

Long seconds passed, and the creature's struggles weakened. Its legs no longer beat against the floor, and its relentless strength no longer pressed against her as hard.

Movement came from beyond the *Chead*. Chris staggered to his feet, his face already turning purple, one eye so swollen she could barely see his hazel eye. Even so, he stumbled forward and fell to his knees beside her. He raised a fist and drove it into the *Chead's* face.

Liz felt the power of Chris's blow through the *Chead*. Its body went limp in her arms, but still she held on, wanting to be sure.

Finally satisfied, she loosened her grip, and with Chris's help, heaved the dead weight from her chest.

Then she was embracing Chris, pulling him to her, clinging desperately at his back. An awful sob built in her chest and escaped in a rush. Chris's arms tightened around her, and then he was sobbing too, his hot wet tears falling on her shoulder.

They clung to each other in silence, and let the horror wash over them.

CHAPTER 23

CHRIS LOOKED up as a door clicked open. Halt stood in the doorway, a triumphant grin stretching across his thin lips. His eyes feasted on the two of them, shining with a wild exaltation.

"It worked," his voice was raw with emotion. He stepped into the room, two guards following behind him before the door swung shut. "The genomes are expressing – a few at least. Muscle density factor, reaction time, agility, it's all there..."

As the man rambled, Chris struggled to pull his mind back to the present. He wrapped his arm around Liz, pulling her tight against him. A shiver went through her and he glanced down, his gaze catching in her crystal eyes.

Then she turned, facing Halt. "What have you done to us?" She croaked.

Halt drew to a stop across from them. He blinked, looking almost surprised, as though he had not expected them to speak. His smile faded as he crossed his arms. "We have enhanced you, my dear. Made you better… made you *useful*," he almost spat the last word.

Chris met the man's iron gaze. "*Why?*" He gestured to the *Chead*. "Why would you do this? Send us in here to die?"

Shaking his head, Halt moved around the room towards the unconscious *Chead*. "To see if you would survive," he answered, looking back at them. "To see if we had succeeded."

His words whispered around the room. Chris's chest contracted and he struggled to breathe. Rage boiled through his veins. He clenched his fist, but pain seared from his knuckles where the *Chead* had held him. Glancing down at his hand, he saw it was already beginning to swell.

A shiver went through him.

It would have killed me.

"You changed us," Liz was speaking again, her voice barely audible. "Did something to us… while we slept. *How?*" Her voice cracked at her final question. She trembled in his arms, though whether from rage or some other emotion, he could not tell.

Chuckling softly, Halt moved back towards them. "It was a simple matter, in the end. A little retrovirus, some genetic mapping of various species – chimpanzees, wolves, felines, eagles, and so on. Isolating the desirable genes took time, as did altering their repetition sequences to be accepted by human cells," he shrugged. "But, well, the results were worth the effort. And the best is yet to come." An awful grin spread across the doctor's face.

With Halt's words, Chris mind finally caught up with events. Revulsion twisted in his stomach as he realised the truth – that the *Chead* had not been weaker than those on the television. No, it was he and Liz who had changed.

And it was Halt who had changed them.

A scream built in Chris's chest as he looked at the doctor. An awful sense of violation wrapped around his throat. He clenched his fist again, felt the pain, but the injury was nothing to the desecration of his body. He felt defiled, like something had been taken from him, stolen by the doctor.

As the pain built in his hand, he drew back his lips in a snarl.

Halt watched them, his expression unchanged, but his hand drifted towards his watch. An awful tension hung in the air as Chris's rage gathered strength.

Then a groan came from across the room, and Halt's eyes flickered towards the *Chead*. Chris followed his gaze and saw the boy had rolled onto his side. He moaned again, then started to cough. His eyes fluttered but did not open.

"It's still alive," Halt sounded surprised. He turned back to Chris. "Kill it."

"What?" Chris blinked, staring at the doctor in disbelief.

"Kill it," Halt repeated. "That monstrosity is not worthy of this earth. Kill it, Christopher. Prove you are superior."

"No." Chris blinked, surprised by his own resolve. Releasing Liz, he faced Halt, determined to defy him. "I won't."

Halt slowly shook his head. He held up his arm. The watch flashed on his wrist, an unspoken threat. "Do not waste my time, Christopher. Kill the *Chead*, and we can move on from this unpleasant business."

A peal of laughter came from beside Chris. Turning, he saw Liz's eyes flash as she took a step towards Halt. "No, Halt. We won't. We're not your creatures, your slaves to do with as you please. Whatever you've done to us, we're still human."

Halt did not move. His eyes flickered for a second to Liz, then back to Chris. "I will give you one last chance. Kill the *Chead*. *Now!*"

"You're the monstrosity, Halt," Chris replied.

"Very well, Christopher." Halt looked at Liz again. "If that is your decision…"

Reaching down, he pressed his finger to the watch.

Chris closed his eyes and braced himself for the pain. Sucking in a breath, he waited for the familiar fire to encircle his throat, to sap the strength from his legs, to lock his muscles in knots of agony.

But it never came.

From his right came a high-pitched scream. Chris spun, his eyes snapping open as the breath caught in his throat. Beside him, Liz crumpled to the ground. The colour fled her face as she clutched desperately at her throat. Her feet drummed against the soft floor and a strangled scream escaped her gaping mouth.

Then she fell silent, her last gasps of air stolen away.

Chris threw himself forward, desperate to reach her, but strong arms grasped him around the waist and hauled him back. Without thinking he lashed out with his elbow, catching the guard in the face, and the hands released him. He glimpsed the man falling backwards, the other stepping towards him, but he was already at Liz's side, reaching out a hand, grabbing at her wrist.

A jolt of electricity flashed between them, and Chris was hurled backwards across the floor.

Coming to rest a few feet away, Chris groaned and struggled to sit up. Across from him, Liz writhed against the soft floor, her back arching, her mouth wide and gasping for air. Her fingers clawed at the skin of her throat, tearing at the collar's metal chain. But there would be no dislodging the steel links.

Halt stepped between them, a grim smile on his serpent lips. "Seventy-five milliamps," he shook his head. "Enough to cause severe muscle contractions, respiratory failure, death."

Behind him, Liz was as pale as a ghost, her throws of agony already growing weaker. Her mouth opened, gasping like a fish out of water. Yet somehow her crystal eyes found his. Shining with tears, they pierced him, conveying her silent command.

Don't give in!

A sob rattled up from Chris's chest as he closed his eyes, unable to watch any longer. Bowing his head, he cradled his shattered fist. Despair rose within him, threatening to overwhelm him.

"*Please!*" His sob rang from the one-way mirror.

A sudden stillness came over the room. Lying on the ground, Chris did not move, unable to look, to witness the consequence of his defiance. So long as he did not look, he could deny the truth.

Liz couldn't be gone, couldn't be dead.

But in his heart, Chris knew he had to face the truth. Blinking back tears, he sucked in a breath and lifted his head.

Liz lay where she had fallen, her limbs splayed out at random angles, the tangles of her hair caught on her face. The collar shone from her neck, the blinking red light unlit.

Staring at her broken body, a pit opened within Chris, a gulf of despair that threatened to swallow him whole. A desperate sob tore from his throat, a cry of anguish, a plea for life. Lifting himself, he began to crawl towards her. He could feel his strength failing, the last drops of energy falling from him, but with a final lunge he reached out and grasped her wrist.

With barely a whisper, Liz's chest moved. A soft cough came from the fallen girl as her eyelids shifted, blinked.

"*What?*" Halt snarled.

Behind him, the door clicked again, as Doctor Fallow pushed her way into the room.

CHAPTER 24

"ENOUGH, HALT," Angela almost tripped over the words as she spoke.

Halt stared back at her, his eyes wide, his surprise already turning to a wild rage. She knew she had crossed a line, defying him now. This time there were no other doctors to back her up – the others were all tending to the surviving candidates from the PERV-A strain of the virus. She shivered, thinking of the room full of candidates, their bodies ravaged by the virus. It had proven far more deadly than the B strain retrovirus the others had been subjected too.

"Excuse me?" Halt sounded almost bemused.

"I said, that's enough," Angela repeated, mustering her courage.

A few moments ago, she had been driven to act. Watching Halt's cruelty, his determination to bend the candidates to his will, had pushed her over the edge. Whatever good she hoped might come from her work, it was not worth this. It was brutal and pointless and wasteful, a display that did nothing more than serve Halt's ego.

And she could not bear to watch the girl die. Angela could not shake that feeling of kinship, could not help but see her own youthful self in the girl's eyes.

So she had acted. She had superseded Halt's controller from within the observation room, disabling the collars inside the room. As supervisor of the Praegressus Project, her watch had precedence over every other controller in the building – even Halt's.

This isn't right, the words whispered in Angela's mind as she glanced at the boy and girl. *They're just kids.*

Biting her lip, she straightened, preparing herself to face Halt's rage. "There was no point to it, Halt. They passed the test. The project is a success. But this," she waved a hand to indicate the girl, "this display is pointless. I won't allow it."

Halt shifted on his feet. A strange calm seemed to have come over him. "You won't allow it?"

Angela found herself retreating a step, though the doctor had not moved. "No," she shook her head. "I've disabled their collars."

"You forget yourself, doctor," Halt still spoke in a soft voice. "These displays of insolence… are becoming problematic."

"They are *my* candidates, Halt."

For a moment, Halt did not reply. His grey eyes studied her, sweeping across her body, cold and calculating. Angela lifted her chin, facing him down.

At last Halt nodded. He waved to the guards. "Get them up. Return them to their cell."

As the guards moved across to Christopher and Elizabeth, Halt turned back to Fallow. He stood deathly still, poised in the centre of the room as the guards shepherded the two experiments from the cells. His eyes did not blink, never left Angela's face. Finally, as the door clicked shut behind the guard, he stepped towards her.

Now Fallow found herself retreating from the rage in the man's eyes. But after two steps she found herself pressed up against the mirror, the cold glass at her back, with nowhere to look but the eyes of the doctor.

Before she could move, Halt's hand flashed out and caught her by the throat. His fingers clenched tight as she opened her mouth to scream, stealing away her voice. His lips drew back in a scowl as he leaned in.

"*How dare you?*" Halt hissed.

With a sudden, violent push, Halt slammed her head back into the glass. Stars spun across Angela's vision and her knees went weak. Pain lanced from her skull as Halt pulled her back towards him, until their faces were less than an inch apart.

"If you *ever* defy me again, I will see you in a cage with your precious candidates," Halt grated.

Red exploded across Angela's vision as he slammed her into the mirror again. Then the fingers released her, and with a muffled sob she slumped to the ground.

Halt looked down at her, open contempt in his eyes. "The experiment will continue," he said. "You will see that the final doses are administered to the candidates. Those still unconscious will remain in their comas until our research has been completed."

Darkness swept across Angela's vision, rising up to claim her. But through the creeping shadows, she heard Halt's final proclamation.

"Succeed, and I might just let you live."

CHAPTER 25

CLANG.

Chris slumped to the ground as the cell door slid closed behind them. Liz staggered past him and toppled onto Ashley's bed. The guards had practically carried her this far. Despite coming out better than Chris in the fight, the collar had left its mark. The damage ran deep, and each inhalation brought about an awful cough and rattling to her chest.

Unfortunately, he wasn't much better.

Whatever Halt had said about success, Chris had still lacked the relentless strength of the *Chead*. When it had caught him, no amount of skill, training or mutated muscle had been enough to save him from its grasp.

Thank God for Liz, he thought, looking across at her.

She lay sprawled across the bed, her face half buried in the pillow, her back rising with each laboured breath. Every few seconds she would groan, but otherwise she lay still.

Getting to his hands and knees, Chris crawled across to Sam's bed and pulled himself up. Under the circumstances, he didn't think the others would mind if they borrowed them. Both beds were neatly made up, the covers pulled tight, the presence of their two friends wiped clean.

Minutes slipped by as he lay there, his face throbbing where the *Chead* had struck him. After a time, the clang of the outer door carried down the corridor. Idly, Chris wondered if someone had come to finish the job the *Chead* had started. There was no one else inside the prison block now. The other cells were empty, the faces that had once lined the corridor either dead or gone.

No, whoever it was had come for them.

Unable to summon the energy to move, Chris lifted an eyelid and looked out into the corridor. A woman stood outside the bars, her hands fiddling nervously with the hem of her lab coat. For a second he thought it was Fallow, before he realised she was too young, her hair blonde instead of brown. A guard stood beside the woman, looking bored.

"I'm... I'm to give you a round of antibiotics," she squeaked.

On the opposite bed, Liz did not so much as stir. Stifling a groan, Chris rolled onto his side. "Really?" he coughed. "You people are all of a sudden concerned for our wellbeing?"

The woman gave a nervous nod. "Could you, could you get to the back of the cell, please?"

Chris blinked. If he hadn't been in so much pain, he would have laughed. Instead he looked at Liz, then back at the doctor. "Sorry, lady. But I don't think we're going anywhere."

"But... but you're meant to..."

Closing his eyes, Chris lay back on the bed. "Just get it over with. Have the guard ready to press his little button, if it makes you feel better."

The woman hesitated another second, and then nodded. A buzzer sounded and the cell door slid open. The little doctor hopped into the cell, a packet of syringes held in one hand, a vial of clear liquid in the other.

Briefly, Chris contemplated the thought of resisting. After everything they'd been through, he distrusted even this harmless-looking woman. Who knew what new horror might wait in the vial. But a hollow feeling sat in his stomach, an awful, helpless weakness that sapped him of the will to resist.

After all, what was the point in fighting now? It was too late – they'd already lost, already been damaged beyond repair.

Chris slumped into his pillow and watched as the woman moved across to Liz.

"She's unconscious," she sounded surprised. "I thought... I thought the experiment was a success."

On the bed, Chris shrugged. "You'll have to ask your boss about that," he paused, his thoughts drifting. "Where are our friends? What's happening to them?"

The woman was busy preparing her syringe, and it was a moment before she answered. It wasn't until she leaned over Liz that he heard her whisper. "The others are being kept in their comas," she breathed. "To make the change easier."

Chris watched as the woman inserted the needle into Liz's back and pressed down the plunger. Then she was moving towards him, the needle disappearing into a bag marked biological waste. Another appeared as she raised the vial.

Turning away, Chris winced as the needle pinched his back. The cold tingle of the injection spread between his shoulder blades as the woman stepped back. To his relief, there was no pain, and the cold sensation quickly faded away.

Chris looked up as footsteps retreated through the cell. He watched the woman reach the door and turn back, her eyes catching in his. "I'm sorry."

Then she was gone.

Frowning, Chris shook his head, resigning himself to whatever fresh torment had been in the injection. He was certain now it had not been antibiotics. Something in her face as she looked back, in those final words, warned him.

At least this time there was no pain.

A gurgled breath came from Liz's bed, drawing his attention back to the girl. She had rolled onto her back now, her mouth wide and gasping. Her eyes were closed, her brow creased as though she were struggling to wake. Fingers clenched at the sheets and the veins stood up against her neck.

Chris's heart lurched and a sense of urgency gripped him. Careful to protect his broken hand, he rolled from the bed and crawled across to the other set of bunks. Pulling himself up beside Liz, he reached for her as she started to thrash. A wild arm swung out, catching him in the face, and a foot struck a pole, making the bunk shake. Another awful gurgle came from her chest.

"Liz, Liz, *stop*," Chris breathed, struggling to calm her.

But with growing fear, he realised what was happening. Liz was choking, drowning in the fluid filling her lungs.

Ignoring the agony in his hand now, Chris reached out and caught Liz as another convulsion took her. He pulled her close, fighting to hold her, to turn her on her side. Desperate fists beat against him, and pain rippled up his arm as she struck his hand. Gasping, he twisted, narrowly avoiding a wild swing of her knee.

Fighting back his pain, Chris heaved, pulling Liz onto her side. As she rolled, he saw her eyes were wide now and staring, though it was clear she still lay in the grips of unconsciousness. Bloodshot veins threaded the whites of her eyes, and a trickle of blood ran from her nose, staining the white of her pillow red.

As she settled onto her side, a ragged gasp tore from her lips. Her chest rose, the gurgle fading to a whispered cough. She gulped again, wheezing in the cool air, as though still unable to get enough oxygen. Reaching out, Chris tilted her head forward slightly, memories of high school first aid returning.

Moving her upper arm, he placed her hand beneath her head, then pulled up her knees. Liz's breathing gradually eased, the gurgle slowly fading as her airways cleared.

Finally, Chris let out a long sigh, satisfied for the moment she was safe. Holding her in place, he sent out a silent thanks that Liz was so small.

Weariness swept through Chris like a wave. He looked across at Liz and smiled. Her eyes had closed again, her lips parted just a fraction, while a wisp of hair fluttered on her face with each exhalation. The sharp throb of his hand was quickly returning though, cutting through the last dredges of adrenaline. He stifled a groan of his own, eager not to disturb Liz now she had settled.

He saw her again in the padded room, thrashing on the floor, felt again the awful helplessness. He shuddered and pushed the image away.

Only Fallow's intervention had saved her, saved them both.

Fallow.

The woman's face drifted through his thoughts. She had been in this from the start, had admitted her role in the facility while they lay in the clean room.

You are the culmination of my life's work.

Was that why she had saved them, had stopped Halt in the padded room? Or was there more? Had the woman's conscience gotten to her?

Chris struggled to concentrate, but cobwebs tangled with his thoughts, and he could make no sense of the questions. His body throbbed, the ache of a hundred bruises dulling his mind. Beside him, heat radiated from Liz, banishing the cold of the cell. Distantly, he felt the pull of sleep.

His eyes fluttered open, catching a glimpse of Liz. The pained twist of her lips had faded, revealing a softness in her face, the kindness of the girl hidden within. Her breathing had quieted now, and her eyes quivered beneath her eyelids, lost in some dream.

The weight of exhaustion slowly dragged Chris's eyes shut again. He knew he should move, should return to the other bed. But the strength would not come; his last ounce of energy had fled.

Within seconds, the soft whispers of sleep claimed him.

CHAPTER 26

LIGHT BURNED at Liz's eyelids, dragging her back from her dreams, back to the pain. It washed over her like rain, a tingle that burned in every muscle, every fibre of her being. Gritting her teeth, she willed the agony to fade, to release her from its fiery grip.

Slowly, the pain died away, slipping from her body, until only embers remained.

Liz sucked in a breath, then suppressed a groan as the ache returned, now an icy frost spreading through her lungs. Whatever damage the collar had inflicted, it had spread to every fibre of her being. It would take more than one night to heal.

Liz froze as movement came from beside her. Cracking open an eye, she found Chris asleep beside her. For a moment she frowned, the beginnings of anger curling in her throat. Then a dim memory came to her, of water all around her, of drowning in a bottomless ocean, of fire in her chest as she breathed the salty water.

Then Chris's firm hands on her shoulders, pulling her up, dragging her to the surface. And the relief of fresh air, filling her lungs, of oxygen flooding her body.

Her anger faded, replaced by a warmth that swept away the pain. She looked at Chris, watching the soft rise and fall of his chest, the flickering of his eyelids. Silently, she remembered her fear as the *Chead* had beaten him to the ground, the terror that had risen within her. But rather than panic, it had filled her with purpose, with the need to act, to save him.

A low moan came from Chris and he wriggled beneath the thin blanket, drawing closer. She sighed as his heat washed over her, and watched as his eyes slowly cracked open.

"You know, when I said I'd give you a chance, I didn't mean it as an invite…" she teased, a playful smile tugging at her lips.

She caught him as he flinched away from her. Taking a gentle hold of his good hand, she pulled him back, drew him close, until only an inch separated them.

"Don't," she murmured, basking in the heat of Chris's body. "Don't."

His hazel eyes stared back at her, streaked with a bloodshot red, but clear and filled with… something. She leaned in, trying to make out what, and her mouth brushed against his. A jolt of energy surged through her at the touch, and then she was kissing him.

She felt Chris tensed against her, and for a second thought he would pull away.

Then his hands were in her hair, and he was kissing her back, his lips hard against hers. A tingle came from her hip as a hand gripped her. Adrenaline throbbed in her chest, spreading to swallow her. She reached out, her arms wrapping around Chris, pulling him closer, leaving no escape. Goosebumps prickled her skin as fingers slid to the small of her back.

Leaning her head back, Liz parted her lips, her tongue flicking out to taste him. The scent of him filled her nostrils as his tongue found hers, and they danced to a rhythm all of their own. Her mind fell away, drowned by the blood rushing from her racing heart. Her pain was forgotten, replaced by threads of pleasure winding through her body. Her skin was aflame, burning wherever his fingers touched.

Reaching up, she slid her fingers through his hair, pulling him deeper. A hunger filled her, a need that grew with every heartbeat. A moan slipped from her lips and she gripped him hard, desperate now.

Chris flinched in her arms and she paused, remembering his broken hand. For a moment they slowed, but their lips did not part, their tongues still touching, tasting. Liz wriggled in under his arm, her chest pounding like a drum as his good arm wrapped around her.

Liz drew back then, sucking in a breath of air. Opening her eyes, she looked at him, saw the smile tugging at his lips. She shivered, a memory rising from her past, the horror of the day before returning. A sour taste filled her mouth, the pain returning. She blinked, and a tear streaked down her cheek.

"What are we doing, Chris?" she whispered.

Chris pulled back, his eyes sad. Reaching up, he wiped away the tear, then kissed her on the forehead. "What do you mean?"

Liz shook her head. "What's the point?" she choked, closing her eyes, the darkness welling within her. "They could kill us tomorrow, mutate us beyond recognition, burn the last traces of humanity from us—"

She broke off as Chris kissed her again, quick and hard. Separating, he looked her in the eye. "We can't let them win, Liz," he whispered. "They've taken so much from us already, used us, stolen our humanity. But they can't take our spirit, our hope. It's like a flame inside me – barely a flicker now, but it keeps me going. It's mine. It's ours. And I won't let them take it."

"Haven't they already?"

Chris only smiled. "Not yet. It's like Ashley said - they're only human. They'll make mistakes." The fingers of his good hand found hers, and squeezed. "When they do, we'll be ready."

Staring into his eyes, Liz could almost bring herself to believe.

Almost.

Still, he was right. They couldn't let their captors win. For the moment, they still had each other. She would not let them take that from her too. Leaning in, Liz gave herself to the flame burning inside her. Their mouths locked and she pressed hard against him, her hands sliding beneath his shirt. A wild hunger filled her, her kisses turning ravenous. His arms went around her again, gripping her with a new fierceness. His lips left hers as he pulled away - then they were pressed against her neck, igniting flames wherever they touched.

She groaned, her neck arching backwards, her fingers tight in his hair.

His hands slid beneath her shirt, trailing across her back, tingling wherever they touched. The warmth inside her spread, and she began to tremble. Lost in her passion, she leaned in and nipped at his neck.

Liz smiled as Chris gave a little yelp. His hands continued to roam, though they had not yet gone far enough for her liking. Reaching up, she slid her fingers through the buttons of his shirt and began to undo them. Beneath, a fine layer of hair covered his chest. His skin burned beneath her fingers.

Chris's mouth found its way to the small of her throat, and with a rush of impatience she helped him with her own buttons, knowing his good hand was already occupied. His lips slid lower, his tongue darting out, tasting her, even as his hands etched invisible trails across the soft skin of her back.

Clutching hard to his arm, Liz stifled a moan as Chris paused. His fingers froze on her back, his mouth's progress coming to an abrupt halt.

Opening her eyes, Liz looked down at him. He stared up at her from between the folds of her breasts, fear sparkling in his hazel eyes. Her stomach twisted as a trickle of ice slid down her back.

"What?" she whispered.

"There's... there's something wrong... There are... lumps..." Chris replied softly.

Liz's cheeks burned, but her fear fell away. Laughing softly, she shook her head. Her hands slid through his hair, drawing him in, until his lips brushed across her.

Chris gave a low groan, then shook his head again. "No," he pulled away, "not... not those," the hackles rose on Liz's neck as he looked at her.

The heat slowly drained from Liz's face. "What?"

"On your back," Chris said, his breath harsh. "There's... something on your back."

Fear flooded Liz, and the passion in her chest spluttered and died. Sitting upright, she craned her neck, straining to see. Her movements grew frantic as she fumbled at her shirt, tugging at the collar, desperate to rid herself of it. Chris reached for her, tried to calm her, but she pushed him away. She heard fabric tear, and then the shirt came loose. Throwing it aside, she twisted her neck again and looked.

Beside her, Chris's face flushed, and his eyes flickered with desire. But she no longer cared, had eyes for only one thing now. Her naked back shone in the fluorescent lights, the lumps clear now. They bulged in the centre of her back, one on either side of her spine, midway between her arms and hips.

A pressure built in Liz's chest and escaped as a low whine, a muffled scream. An awful horror swept through her, a raging anger at the doctors, at their violation of her body. Another shriek built, but she swallowed it down, blinking back tears.

Her eyes burned as she looked at Chris, saw the fresh tears in his eyes.

"Where does it stop?" she whispered.

CHAPTER 27

WITHIN HOURS, Chris found a pair of growths on his own back. Though there was no pain or discomfort, they ignited a terrible horror inside him, a building terror that threatened to overwhelm him. Whatever the doctors had done to them, it seemed they had failed after all.

They made a mistake, the words whispered through his thoughts, along with something else, a familiar word, a horror from his childhood.

Cancer.

The memory of his father's illness still lay heavy on his mind – the wasting sickness, the slow loss of strength, of life. Despite its ferocity, his father had fought back, had even won, for a time. But cancer was like a weed, always there, waiting to return. It wore you down, drew the life from you one drop at a time.

And his father, once larger than life, had been laid low.

Now as the hours ticked past, Chris watched with

horror as the lumps on his back grew. It could only be cancer. Vicious and unrelenting, it would spread through their bodies, poisoning their blood, robbing them of strength, until there was nothing left but empty husks.

Lying on the bed, he held Liz in his arms, each alone in their own thoughts.

The next day, they woke to the first pangs of pain. It began as a soft twitch from the centre of his back, radiating outwards from the strange protrusions. The ache pulsed, flickering with the beat of his heart, but growing sharper with each intake of breath. Hour by hour it spread across his back, threaded its way into his chest, until it hurt just to breathe.

For Liz, it was worse. When she woke she could barely speak. Her skin had lost its colour, even the angry red marks beneath her collar had paled to white. By lunch she could no longer lie on her back. When he touched a hand to her forehead, her skin was burning hot with fever.

Each hour the lumps grew. Their skin stretched and hardened around the protrusions, darkening to purple bruises. Each bulge was unyielding to their scrutinising prods, and soon tiny black spots appeared on their surface.

When the lights flickered on the morning of the third day, Chris could hardly move from the pain. Agony wove its way through his torso, spreading out like the roots of a tree, engulfing his lungs, reducing each breath to a battle, a desperate fight for life.

The next time a guard arrived with food, Chris

could no longer tell whether it was breakfast or dinner. Forcing open his eyes, he blinked hard in the light, pain lancing through his skull. The room spun and then settled into a double image of two guards. His stomach churned as two images of Liz stood over him and offered a bowl of dark looking stew. He saw her waver on her feet, and blindly took the bowl before she fell.

Sitting back, he raised a shaking spoonful of broth to his mouth, but there was no taste when he swallowed. His stomach swirled again, then he began to heave. He barely made it to the toilet. A moment later Liz was at the sink beside him.

Afterwards, Chris slid to the ground, his head throbbing in the blinding light. Liz slumped beside him, her head settling on his shoulder. For a moment the pain faded, giving in to a wave of warmth. He closed his eyes, savouring Liz's closeness, but the relief did not last long. His stomach lurched again and releasing Liz he crawled back to the toilet.

The click of the lights going out was a welcome relief.

Stomach clenched, lungs burning, head thumping, Chris crawled back to the beds. Stars danced across his vision, but he hauled himself into a bed, no longer caring who's it was. The room stank of vomit and spilt food, of unwashed bodies and blood. The scent of chlorine had long since been overwhelmed.

Caught in the clutches of fever, Chris lost all track of time. At some point he felt Liz's body beside him, though he could not recall whose bed they slept in.

His fevered mind drew comfort from the heat of her presence, in the closeness of her face. Then her face warped, his own body distorting, and he forced his eyes closed.

Wild colours spun through his mind as time passed. At one point he remembered calling out, begging the guards to help them, to bring the doctors, to bring anyone. But no one came, no one responded, and he soon stopped asking for help. A short while later, he started asking for death.

In his dreams, he saw his body slowly decaying, watched his veins turn black with death, his arms begin to rot. Then he would find himself whole, riding in the passenger seat of his father's 68 Camaro, his dad driving, an infectious grin on his youthful face. A moment later he was in a hospital, the smell of bleach and beeping of machinery all around. And his father lay in a bed, his arms withered, his face lined with age. Only the smile remained the same.

Again the image faded, and Chris was back in the cell, back with the pain. Looking at his arms, he wondered what was real, what was not. One instant it was night, the next the blinding light of day, then back to black. At times he would wake, gasping for air, shivering beneath the blanket, and know in his heart he was dying.

Once, he dreamed that he was flying, that he was soaring through mountains, far from the nightmares of their prison cell.

And then he woke.

CHAPTER 28

IT TOOK a long time for Chris to decide he was no longer dreaming. The cold air wrapped around him, sending a shiver through him, but otherwise there was no discomfort. The pain had vanished, and for a second he considered the possibility he was dead. Then a low groan came from someone nearby, and he knew he was not alone.

Squeezing open his eyes, he peered out from the shadows of his bunk bed, searching for Liz.

The first thing he realised was that they had not been alone in their fever dreams. Someone had entered the room while they slept, cleaning the mess of vomit and blood that had stained the room. Liz lay in the opposite bed, covered now by a blanket of black feathers. She shifted beneath it, then blinked across at him, raising a hand to shield her face. Her lips parted, her tongue licking her cracked lips.

"Chris?" she croaked.

"I'm here," he replied, his throat raw. A desperate

thirst clutched him, and he looked across at the sink, wondering if he had the strength to reach it.

In the other bed, Liz shifted, the blanket of feathers moving with her. Dimly, Chris made to do the same, but a weight on his back pushed him down. Reaching back, the soft points of feathers brushed his hand. He shrugged, trying to dislodge the blanket, and struggled to his hands and knees.

Chris paused, a distant thought tugging at his memories. Before he could catch it, it faded into the darkness. He looked across at Liz, eyes questioning, but she had fallen silent. He clenched his fists, feeling a wrongness about himself, but unable to trace its source.

Shaking his head, Chris pushed the last of the fever dreams from his mind and rolled out of the bed onto his feet. To his shock, the weight came with him, pushing him forward. Off-balance, he crashed to the floor in a tangle of limbs and feathers.

"Chris?" Liz's voice shook.

Head spinning, Chris looked up from the floor, unable to understand what had happened. Confused, he pulled himself up, but the weight still clung to his back. Only sheer determination kept him from toppling over again. Looking at Liz, he froze at the look on her face.

Liz sat half-crouched on the bed, eyes wide. Her mouth opened and closed, but no sound came out. Her arm shook as she raised it and pointed. Shivering, he looked back, fear of the unknown rippling down his spine. But his bed was empty, the feather blanket trailing out behind him.

Chris blinked, started to turn back towards Liz, then paused. He blinked again, staring at the tawny brown feathers of his blanket. There was something wrong about the way they hung between himself and the bed, something not quite right.

Stretching out a hand, Chris tried to dislodge the blanket from his shoulders. He flinched as his hand brushed against something unexpected, something hard beneath the blanket. Withdrawing his hand, he looked at Liz, but she only sat in silent shock, her mouth still agape.

Holding his breath, Chris reached behind his neck and ran a hand down his spine.

He found the growths where they had been before, midway down his back. But they had grown now, changed, becoming long shafts that stretched out beyond his reach. A soft down of feathers covered their length, sprouting from his flesh as though they had every right to be there.

Wings.

His mind spun. He shook his head, refusing to face the truth, though they lay stretched out before his eyes. He trembled, and watched the shiver run down the wings, the tawny brown feathers quivering in the cool air.

He turned as a muffled sob came from the other bed. Liz had struggled to her feet, revealing the long black wings hanging from her back. They stretched out either side of her, each at least ten feet long, the large black feathers tangling with the sheets on the bed. Where the feathers bent, Chris glimpsed soft white down beneath, small feathers curled in upon themselves, gripping close to her flesh. The feathers shone in the overhead lights, seeming almost aflame, as though Liz was some avenging angel descended from heaven.

Wings.

Warmth spread through Chris's chest to mingle with the horror. A profound confusion gripped him; a disgust at this fresh violation, the further loss of his humanity – but also wonder, an awe for the trembling new limbs on his back.

Wings.

He looked at Liz. Her eyes were wide, glistening with tears. Her lips trembled as a shudder ran through her body. Through her wings.

For the first time he realised they were both naked. Strangely, that no longer seemed to matter. After all they had suffered, all that had been done to them, Chris's body hardly felt like his own. He felt apart from it now, separated from his nakedness.

A tear spilt down Liz's cheek, and he knew the same thoughts were filling her mind. He stepped across, struggling for balance, and drew her to him. He shivered as her arms went around his waist and her head leaned back, drawing him in.

A fire ignited in Chris's chest as their lips met. His hands slid up into her hair as her tongue darted out, sliding between his lips. The taste of her filled his mouth, and the intoxicating scent of her hair toyed with his nostrils.

After a long minute, Liz pulled back. Raising a hand to her face, she wiped away her tears. Turning, she looked at her wings, her lips twisting in thought. They hung limply from her back, feathers quivering, and he knew what she was thinking.

Sucking in a breath, Liz closed her eyes. Her face tightened, the muscles of her jaw deepening. Her brow creased, and behind her the black-feathered wings gave a twitch. Then they began to shake, lifting slightly and half opened. There they paused, as though lacking the strength for more.

Liz bit her lip, her eyes still closed, and persisted.

And bit by bit, her wings spread, until they seemed to fill the cell. Combined, they stretched more than twenty feet wide, twice the length of the beds, so that their tips poked out through the bars into the corridor.

Twenty feet of jet-black feathers, of curly white down, of a majestic, undefinable magic.

When Liz opened her eyes again, Chris saw the wonder there, the fear falling away before it.

At a nod from her, he shut his own eyes and sought to do the same. Reaching down into the depths of his consciousness, he followed the tingle that came from his back, from the newfound limbs hanging across his bed. As he concentrated, the tingle spread along his spine. The hairs stood up on his neck as new connections formed within his mind, as neurons flared into life, recognising the presence of new muscles and bone and flesh.

A tremor went through the weight on his back. There was a wrongness to that weight, an awkward presence to it, like clothes that did not quite fit. But opening his mind, he sought to accept it, to embrace it.

At last, Chris opened his eyes. A sharp crack tore the air as his wings snapped open, unfurling to fill the room. Feathers as long as his forearm brushed against the far wall, touched the bars of the cell, and he *felt it*, sensed the pressure against his feathers.

Turning, he grinned at Liz, unable to keep the wonder from his face. She grinned, laughed, opened her arms to embrace him.

Then with a deafening shriek, an alarm began to sound.

CHAPTER 29

Angela strode around the corner and started towards the wide iron door at the end of the corridor. Heavy locking bars stretched across the dull metal, and a guard stood to either side, watching her approach. Each held a heavy rifle and wore the familiar trigger watches on their wrists. With a flick of their fingers, the men could activate any collar in their immediate vicinity, incapacitating any threat the prisoners within might pose.

Or at least, that was the idea.

Today, the watches had been reduced to worthless pieces of steel and glass. Just ten minutes before, Angela had entered her code to deactivate all the collars inside the facility. Halt, in his arrogance, had thought her cowed by his violence.

Instead, Angela had resolved to act.

Left alone in the padded room, fading in and out of consciousness, Angela had finally seen the true futility of her research. It had never been about a cure, or a weapon to fight the *Chead*. It had always been about *this*, this need for power, for a weapon against their enemies.

And Angela knew, threats or no, she could not allow the Praegressus project to continue.

Climbing to her feet, the weight of regret heavy on her shoulders, Angela had settled on a new path.

Now the time had come to act, and she knew she could not hesitate.

Ahead, the guards pulled back the heavy bolts, and with a screech, the iron door swung open. Angela walked past the guards without breaking stride, nodding as she went.

Inside, a hushed silence gathered over the narrow corridor as a dozen faces turned towards her. Another screech and the door swung shut, sealing her inside. Taking a breath, she started forward, careful to keep to the centre of the hall, beyond the reach of grasping arms.

Hard grey eyes followed her passage.

Tension hung like a blanket on the air as she made her way past the cells. Hate permeated the air, radiating from the dark creatures pressing up against the prison bars. There were twelve in all: six boys, six girls.

Twelve vicious killing machines, hungry for blood, for freedom.

The *Chead* watched her as she reached the corridor's end and turned back. Each had been born in the facility. Each was destined to die here. These creatures would never feel the heat of the sun, nor the cold of snow. Their eyes would never see the beauty of the mountains beyond the walls, their ears would never hear the roar of ocean waves.

Or at least, that was Halt's plan.

Each of the *Chead* wore the familiar steel collars on their neck. Each of those collars were now little more than decorative necklaces.

Standing at the end of the corridor, Angela faced the exit. The cells stretched out either side of her, the males to her left, females to her right. Something about the change accelerated the development and reproductive drive of the *Chead*. Left to their own devices, they bred like rabbits. And though the occupants of the cells appeared fully mature, the oldest was just ten years old.

Stealing herself, Angela walked back towards the exit. The grey eyes followed her, alive with intelligence, searching for an opportunity. One second, one slip, was all they needed. Several men had lost their lives by wandering too close to the bars. Angela would not make that mistake.

But she needed them to see her, to be awake.

To be ready.

As she approached the entrance, the guard by the door reached out to open it. She gazed at his face for a moment as she passed, a flicker of guilt swelling within her. But it was too late for regrets now. It was time.

As the door reached its apex, Angela looked down at her watch. It was more advanced than the others, controlled more than just the candidate's collars. As head geneticist and supervisor of the Praegressus project, she had control over many of the security protocols for the facility. That was how she had stopped Halt earlier, and what she planned to use now.

Angela pressed her finger to the touch screen.

Behind her, a buzzer began to screech, followed by the rattling of cell doors opening. Angela leapt forward as the guards looked up, confusion sweeping across their faces. They stared, eyes wide with bewilderment, as Angela stepped past them and began to run.

The screams of the dying chased her down the corridor.

———

Angela's breath came in ragged gasps as she took a corner. From behind her came the roar of gunfire and the growls of the *Chead*. Overhead, lights flashed, and somewhere in the building a siren screeched. Muffled voices came from speakers at intervals down the corridors, a robotic voice asking her not to panic.

The thump of approaching boots came from ahead. She tensed as two guards raced into view, then relaxed as they sprinted past, guns held at the ready. Their eyes barely registered her, but she saw their fear. Just as well. With a dozen *Chead* loose in the building, they would be hard-pressed to survive.

A minute later she drew up outside the other prison block. She had hesitated before detouring there

– only two of the seven survivors were located there. But the face of the girl had risen in her mind, and Angela knew she could not abandon her.

Fortunately, the guards had already abandoned their posts – though whether to face the *Chead* or run, she wasn't sure. The door to the cell block had been left open, and she stepped inside, shivering as her eyes swept over the rows of empty cells.

So much loss.

Angela closed her eyes, regret welling up within her. How had she been so blind? She had allowed her ambition to surpass caution, to blind her to the atrocities within the facility. Her morals, her integrity, all had been lost before her drive to succeed.

And these children had paid the price.

Moving down the corridor, Angela searched for the two she had come for. She froze when she found them, her breath catching in her throat.

She had seen them in their fever induced sleep, seen the others in their comas. She already knew the experiment had succeeded; that the homeotic genes had taken. Once stimulated, they acted like a master switch, triggering the cluster of genes embedded in the candidates' genomes. The genes corresponding to wing growth.

Angela had watched the wings grow, watched the feathers sprout like seedlings from their skin. Even so, she was not prepared for the sight that greeted her.

Elizabeth and Christopher stood in all their glory, wings spread wide, stretching out to fill the cell. They had found the ragged clothes she'd left by their beds, with the clumsy holes she'd torn in the backs. The girl's black feathers pressed against the brown of the boy's, their wings entwining in the tiny space.

Angela's heart ached with the wonder of it.

"What's happening?" Christopher demanded.

Blinking, Angela tore herself from her stupor. She shook her head, then looked down at her watch and pressed a button. The cell slid open with a dull rattle.

The two of them stood still, a wary surprise spreading across their faces.

"Come on," Angela said. "We're getting out of here. Hurry, the others should be awake by now."

Christopher's hand drifted to his neck, his fingers touching the collar. Angela shook her head and reached into her pocket. "I've deactivated them," finding the little key, she drew it out and tossed it to them. "Here, that'll unlock them. But *hurry*."

A few seconds later their collars lay discarded on the ground. Angela watched them embrace, saw the tears shining in their eyes, but she could not pause to celebrate their freedom. Apprehension nibbled at her stomach, an awful fear they would be caught.

"*Come on*," she urged again, waving them towards the door. "We need to find the others."

Their eyes widened then, their mouths opening in question, but she was already moving away. Sirens still sounded and red lights flashed in the ceiling, but there was no sign of movement as they moved out into the corridors. The guards remained preoccupied at the other end of the facility, and she hoped the other civilians would have already retreated to the safe room.

Silently she led them through the maze of the facility, to the clean room where the other survivors of the PERV-B strain had remained in their comas. She had swapped out their medication that morning, replacing the drugs with saline. They would be awake by now, and she hoped they had not wandered from the room while she detoured.

Unfortunately, the remaining PERV-A candidates were lost to her. They still lay in their comas, their bodies wracked by fever, struggling to accept the chromosomal alterations of the virus. There was nothing she could do for them now.

Ahead, the door to the clean room lay unguarded. She smiled, glad her distraction had proven so effective. With luck, they would be long gone before anyone realised they were missing. If the guards even managed to regain control of the facility. She had seen a single *Chead* tear a man to pieces. With twelve… she didn't like to think what twelve *Chead* might be capable of.

But there was no more time to think of that. Pushing open the door, Angela led the others inside.

CHAPTER 30

LIZ STUMBLED through the door after Chris. Every step was a struggle to keep upright. The new weight on her back threw her whole coordination out of sync, leaving her feeling strangely out of proportion. Even the simple act of closing her wings had taken several attempts, but she and Chris had finally managed to pull them tight against their backs. Even so, they niggled at her consciousness, an alien presence that would not go away.

The thought of freedom drove her on, the knowledge that each step carried her closer to a possible reunion with Ashley and Sam fuelling her. She sucked in a breath, joying again in the feel of her naked neck. The collar was gone, her throat free of its steel encasing. It felt like a lifetime ago since the awful contraption had trapped her. Perhaps it was.

Blinking, Liz returned her mind to the present. Looking around, she recognised it as the room they had awoken in before. The beds still lined its length, but they were empty now. The whir of machines filled the air, their tubes and wires dangling free. Her chest contracted as her eyes swept the room, searching for her friends.

A thud came from their right, and she spun, raising her fists to defend herself.

Then lowered them. Beside her Chris chuckled, as together they watched the figure sprawled on the ground struggling to sit up.

It took a few seconds for Sam to get his tangle of limbs and copper wings under control, and several more before he managed to stand. A string of curses echoed from the walls as he finally pulled himself up, red in the face, puffing like he'd run a marathon. Then her eyes drifted past Sam, and she gave a wild yelp.

Ashley strode forward, her lips twitching with suppressed humour. She moved with the same casual grace as before, her lithe legs easily finding their balance as she weaved between the empty beds. Trailing out behind her, a pair of snow-white wings shone in the overhead lights. They quivered as she moved, slowly lifting from the ground, expanding across the room.

Liz laughed again as Ashley reached her, then stepped up to draw the girl into a hug. They clung to each other for a moment, arms gripped tightly. When they finally broke apart, Ashley's eyes travelled past Liz. She raised an eyebrow at the doctor.

When Fallow did not speak, Ashley nodded and turned back to Liz. "I guess we found their weakness."

Chris shrugged. "She found us."

The distant wail of sirens prickled at Liz's ears, reminding her they were not out of danger yet. Before she could speak though, another movement came from the far side of the room. Her eyes trailed past Sam and found the remaining survivors of the Praegressus project.

Her heart sank as her eyes alighted on Richard and Jasmine. Their attitude towards the four of them did not appear to have changed in the untold weeks they'd lain unconscious. They still stood on the far side of the room, arms crossed and eyes hard with suspicion. Though it was not their faces that drew her attention. Their wings lay half-furled behind them, each sporting an array of dark emerald feathers, like those of some tropical parrot. Their eyes caught hers and she quickly looked away, unable to face their unspoken accusations, their hate that she was alive, while Joshua was gone.

Of course, she thought. *Of everyone else who could have survived, it would be Richard and Jasmine...*

Well, Richard and Jasmine, and the girl.

Standing beside them was a young girl of maybe thirteen years. Locks of grey hair tumbled around her face, where eyes wide with fear stared out at them. A button nose and freckled cheeks only served to make her look younger – how she had survived this far, Liz couldn't begin to guess. Liz shivered as the girl's eyes, one blue, the other green, found her from across the room.

Looking away, Liz cast her gaze around the room one last time, searching for the others. There had still been dozens of candidates left the last time she had been there. Now there was only the seven of them, each sporting the plain grey uniforms they'd found at the ends of their beds.

"Where are the others?" she whispered, turning to face Fallow.

Fallow looked away, head bowing. When she did not respond, Chris repeated her question. "Doctor Fallow, where are the rest of them?"

Fallow looked back, her eyes flashing. "Don't call me that. I don't deserve to be called 'doctor' after what I've done. My name is Angela." She bowed her head. "And the others did not survive. The physiological changes… they were too much for their bodies to support. Even unconscious, the accelerated wing growth was too much. Their hearts gave out from the strain."

An awful anger spread through Liz as she stepped in close to the doctor. Fallow flinched, but this time she did not look away. "How many did you kill?" Liz hissed.

Angela Fallow closed her eyes. "I've lost count," her eyes snapped open again. "But it ends here. I won't let them take you too."

Liz might have struck her if Chris had not placed a hand on her shoulder. Looking back at him, she saw the sadness in his eyes, the same sorrow from which her own rage spawned. Stepping away from Angela, she hugged Chris to her. A second later she smiled as Ashley joined them, then Sam.

"Ahem." Liz looked up at a new voice. Richard raised an eyebrow. Reaching up, he tapped his collar. "Someone care to share the key?"

Chris nodded. Reaching into his pocket he pulled out the little key Angela had given them and handed it over. The clink of the thick steel collars striking the concrete quickly followed as the five of them freed themselves.

"Are you okay there, Sam?" Chris asked as Sam finally managed to unlock the clasp of his collar.

Sam cursed beneath his breath and tossed the collar aside. "Almost," he said as a shiver went through his copper feathers.

Slowly his wings contracted. "Don't know what the idiots were thinking, putting these clunky things on our backs," he paused, eying Angela uncertainly. "Err, no offence, Doc– I mean, Angela?"

Angela shook her head, a sad smile touching her lips. "And it's alright. You have every right to complain. I would have… I would have stopped them before they gave you the injection, but I was unconscious. Then I had to wait… wait until you were conscious again."

"It's okay." Of all of them, Ashley seemed the best adapted to the new appendages. She looked over her shoulder, smiling. "I kind of like them."

"Yeah," Sam's voice was gruff, but he continued with his usual humour, "but yours are tiny. Did you have to make mine so *big?*"

Angela raised a hand to her mouth, trying to hide her smile. "It took some research of various avian species to get our specifications right. We looked at genome variations between species such as the Andean Condors and Wandering Albatross, then used them to identify genes relating to size in fragmented DNA from *Argentavis magnificens*."

"Argentavis what?" Richard growled from nearby.

"The largest known bird to have flown," Liz looked around as Jasmine spoke.

Angela nodded. "It could weigh up to two-hundred-fifty pounds. Once we'd identified all the genes related to wing surface area, we linked them with those that controlled your own sizes and weights. Thus, why yours are so... big, Samuel."

Sam glanced at Liz. "I think she's calling me fat..."

Smiling, Liz looked around the little group, a strange elation rising within her. Even with the open animosity of Jasmine and Richard, there was a connection between the seven of them now, a shared experience which could not be denied. Of all the desperate souls who had passed through this place, they alone had survived.

They alone had evolved.

And now they needed to get out.

As though reading Liz's mind, Angela turned away from the group and started towards the door. The others paused a moment to collect themselves. Feathers rustled as wings were slowly furled, and then Chris started after her, Liz close behind.

Ahead of them, Angela was stretching out a hand to open the door, when it suddenly swung inwards to meet her.

And Halt stepped into the room.

CHAPTER 31

LIZ FROZE as Halt took a step into the room, the others following suit behind her. Her heart plummeted into the pit of her stomach as his eyes swept the room, his confusion turning quickly to rage. Before any of them could react, they settled on Angela. He clutched a handgun in one hand, and with a snarl, he sprang.

Angela managed a scream before he was on her, his arm wrapping around her waist, spinning her against him. Pressing the gun to her head, he drew back his lips.

"What do we have here, doctor?" he snarled. Angela flinched as he shifted the gun, jabbing it into her ribs. "Have you betrayed me? Have you betrayed us all?"

Clenching her fists, Liz inhaled, tasting the scent of gunpowder on the air. Halt's gun had already been fired recently; the man posed no idle threat. She froze as his eyes turned back to them. A cold grin twisted his lips as Angela struggled in his grasp.

"*That's enough!*" he snapped.

Halt swung the gun, catching Angela in the forehead. She slumped in Halt's hands as he turned back to them. "Don't come any closer."

Liz suppressed a moan. Angela had gone limp now, her amber eyes wide and staring. Her hands swiped feebly at the arms holding her, but Halt was more than a match for the small woman. Biting her lip, Liz flashed a glance at the others. Her arms trembled, the sensation spreading through her body, down her spine, to the foreignness of her wings. A phantom ache started in her throat, the distant reminder of the collar pressing against her flesh.

I won't go back.

She flinched as her fingernails bit the palms of her hands. Drawing in a deep breath, she unclenched her hands, trying to calm herself, to find a way out of the trap. Her eyes travelled across the space separating her from Halt and Angela.

Too far.

But Chris was closer, and from the corner of her eyes, she saw him slide another step towards the doctors. If he could reach her…

No, it was still too far.

Her eyes turned back to Angela. Emotion washed over the doctor's face – fear, anger, regret. Her head sagged as her eyes closed, her whole body trembling. Then her head snapped up, and a new resolve now shone from her eyes. The fear had vanished, replaced by an implacable determination.

Liz opened her mouth to shout, but she was too late. She wasn't sure what she would have said anyway. Would she have begged Angela not to act? Or had she only wanted to thank her, for finally freeing them.

Either way, Liz never got the chance. Still clutched in Halt's arms, Angela jerked her arm and jumped, driving her weight backwards into Halt. Small as she was, the act was enough to throw Halt off balance, and cursing, he staggered backwards.

In that instant, Chris leapt, charging across the ten feet still separating them. He closed the gap in a second, his wings cracking as they beat the air, driving him on. He raised a fist and snarled as he swung it at the doctor. Another second, and it would be over.

The roar of the gun was so sudden, so deafening in the sealed room that Liz found herself stumbling backwards.

Then Chris barrelled into Halt, his fist catching the man in the face. The blow sent Halt hurtling back-wards through the air. He struck the concrete with a dull thud, bounced once then smashed hard against the wall. A low groan came from him as he slumped down and lay still. The gun slid across the floor, coming to rest in a nook between the floor and the wall.

Chris landed lightly on his feet, wings still outstretched, eyes locked on the doctor. But Liz was already moving, running forward, falling to her knees beside Angela. A dark pool spread around her, the overhead lights glimmering on its scarlet surface. Her eyes were open, staring at the ceiling, her mouth wide in a silent scream. One hand still clutched at her chest, where a small red mark stained her lab coat.

Liz knelt over her, staring at the hole through blurry eyes. A low moan came from her throat as she reached out and shook the woman. She heard the soft pad of footsteps from behind her, but she took no notice.

Disbelief threaded around her mind. Whatever her crimes, Angela Fallow had been the only one in this place to show any compassion for them. Twice she had stopped Halt's torture, and in the end, she had followed her conscience, had freed them from the cells.

And now she was dead.

A terrible rage rose in Liz's chest, driving her to her feet. Spinning, she leapt at Halt, crossing the room in a single bound. She reached down and grasped him by the front of his coat, hauling him to his feet. Without effort she lifted him into the air, held him aloft, and then slammed him into the wall.

He groaned, his eyelids flickering, but did not wake. Gritting her teeth, Liz drew back a fist.

Ashley's hand caught her arm before the blow could fall. Liz half-turned, straining against the other girl, a snarl twisting her lips. Frustration built inside her and she spun, dropping Halt to the ground and swung at Ashley.

Ashley leaned back and Liz's blow found only

open air. Her other hand shot out, catching Liz in the chest, pushing her back. Stumbling, Liz straightened and then leapt at her. Rage burned in her throat, filling her with a need to rend, to tear the flesh from her enemies.

"*Liz!*" Ashley screamed, raising an arm to protect herself.

The scream gave Liz pause, and she drew back. Blood pounded in her head, and a voice screamed for her to attack, but she sucked in a breath. Slowly she looked around, blinking back the red haze, and saw the fear dancing in the eyes of the others. She sucked in another mouthful of air, and faced Ashley.

"*Why?*" she asked, her voice breaking. "Why did you stop me?"

"He's not worth it," Ashley breathed. "He's not worth it, Liz. Don't let this place make you like them. Don't let it corrupt you."

Liz clenched her fists, trembling with the effort to suppress her rage. Red flashed across her vision as she turned to look down at Halt, but she fought back the impulse to reach for him.

She bowed her head. "He'll come for us," she whispered.

"They'll come for us anyway," Chris replied, placing a hand on her shoulder. "Besides, I doubt he'll be doing anything after this. They were always talking about needing results," he waved a hand at the room, "and this seems about the opposite of that."

Slowly, Liz allowed her body to relax. She looked up at Chris and nodded.

He stepped forward then, arms open, drawing her to him. They stood there in silence, holding each other, the others forgotten for a second, the nightmare around them a distant memory.

When they finally parted, Liz and Chris turned to face the others. Ashley and Sam, Richard and Jasmine, and the strange little girl stared back. Their eyes shone with emotion: hope mixed with anger, love with hate. Shivering, Liz looked at Chris.

"Let's go."

CHAPTER 32

THE TIRED HINGES of the door screeched as Chris threw himself against it. His shoulder throbbed, and his wings gave a little flap, but on the next blow the door caved. He stumbled after it, his momentum carrying him outside, where a blast of icy air caught in his wings and hurled him backwards. Pain shot from his bare feet as they stumbled on stones. Dropping to his knees, he braced himself against the howling wind, and glanced back at the others.

They filed out after him, one by one, their eyes alight with wonder. Turning, Chris looked out across a world blanketed in white. Flakes of snow swirled around them, drifting ever downwards, their intricate patterns catching in the light shining down from overhead. Clouds covered the sky, but after so long inside, it still seemed impossibly bright. Blinking back tears, Chris watched as the world opened around him.

Rocky mountains stretched up above them, sprouting like enormous trees from the slope on which they stood. Sheer escarpments of rock raced upwards, disappearing into the clouds overhead. A sheen of white covered their frozen surface, but further down the valley the snow and ice gave way to barren rock.

Around the facility there was no sign of trees or vegetation, only jagged gravel that promised to make walking difficult. They had not stopped to search for better clothing or boots, and now Chris shivered as the icy air tore through his thin clothes. A dull ache began at the back of his skull, though despite their now undoubted height above sea level, his breath came easily now.

Turning, Chris stared up the valley, his eyes trailing over the snow-covered boulders, up to where the slope disappeared into a narrow gorge. Glancing back, he studied the valley as it fell away from the facility. There was not a sliver of cover in sight. Even so, down was tempting. Down would bring them to warmer air, out of the mountains, towards civilisation. Perhaps they could find someone to help them, to protect them from the monsters that would hunt them.

But even as he considered the temptation, Chris dismissed it. They would not make it far in that direction. Lower down the clouds cleared, and their pursuers would expect them to take that route. The chase would be over before it began.

No, they needed to do the unexpected. They needed to go higher.

The others gathered behind him, huddling close, wings wrapped tight to fend off the frigid air. Turning to face them, Chris's wings extended of their own accord, curving around to encase him. The relief was instant. The cold creeping through his chest vanished.

The others watched him, wonder and fear mingling on their faces. They all knew the next few hours would decide whether they lived or died. Whatever Angela had done to distract the guards, it could not keep them busy forever. Before long, Halt would wake and the guards would come for them. Chris wanted to be far away by then.

Quickly he explained his plan, watching as Liz, Sam and Ashley nodded. Richard and Jasmine only stood in sullen silence, their faces expressionless. Beside them, the young girl hovered on the edge of the circle. So far they hadn't gotten a word from her. She huddled in close to Jasmine, a nameless, unknown quantity. Not for the first time, he wondered how she had survived.

He'd thought the other two would argue, but they nodded when he finished. "Let's go then," Richard said abruptly.

With a sigh of relief, Chris turned and began the long trek up towards the canyon. He moved as fast as the jagged gravel allowed him, wincing as each step sent a jagged bolt of pain through his feet. Silently he cursed their haste. Boots would have saved them time out in the mountains, but there was no going back now. Glancing around, he made sure the others were following and pressed on.

Half an hour passed as they made their slow way up. The wind howled around them, threatening to hurl them from the rocky slope, but they continued, wings pulled tight against their backs. Briefly Chris considered whether they should attempt to use them, but quickly dropped the thought. Conditions were not ideal for a first attempt at flight.

When they finally reached the canyon mouth, Chris paused, glancing back as the other filed up behind him. One by one they joined him in the shadow beneath the cliffs. Beyond, the canyon twisted deeper into the mountains. A river flowed along its far side, and the roaring of water echoed around them.

The hairs on his neck tingled as Chris looked back down the valley, and saw the black-garbed figures of men spilling from the building below. They gathered near the high walls, concentrating around a man in white. Blinking, Chris watched the distant figures come suddenly into focus. It was as though a film had been removed from his eyes, revealing the world around him in a detail he had never experienced. In that moment he saw them all in crystal clarity, saw the fear in their eyes as they looked at one another, the sleek black steel of their rifles, the blood and tears marking their clothes.

Between them, Halt stood with shoulders hunched, gesturing weakly with his arms. The men did not appear to have seen their little group yet, but it would only take a glance to reveal their position. Silently Chris waved for the others to get into cover, not trusting his voice, in case it carried down to the men below. Turning, he scrambled up the last few feet of the gravel slope, and into the canyon.

The others quickly joined him, scrambling over the lip one by one and dropping out of sight. They retreated behind the boulders lodged in the mouth of the pass, their eyes on Chris, waiting for him to speak.

Heart pounding in his chest, Chris slipped out from behind the boulders. Dropping low, he half-scrambled back up to the gravel lip. At the entrance to the pass, he dropped to his stomach and crawled the last few inches. Then he slowly lifted his head and peered down at the facility.

And immediately dropped back down.

CHAPTER 33

CHRIS SLAMMED a fist into the gravel, cursing their luck.

Just a few more seconds, and we would have been clear.

He slid back down the slope to the others. Biting back his frustration, he only shook his head at their questioning looks. Below, a line of black figures were streaming their way up towards the pass, waved on from behind by the figure in white.

They had been spotted. Now all they could do was flee, and hope to outrun their pursuers.

"They've seen us," he hissed. Moving quickly past them, he began to thread his way through boulders strewn across the floor of the canyon. "Halt's with them. Let's go."

He caught a glimpse of Liz, her eyes shimmering with anger, and looked away. He could not blame her for her rage. Maybe she'd been right – maybe they should not have spared the man's life. But even with Angela lying dead at their feet, he could not bring himself to believe killing Halt in cold blood was the right thing to do.

Either way, it was too late to second guess the decision now.

Gritting his teeth against the wind howling through the canyon, Chris picked his way over the rocky ground, taking care to avoid the patches of ice. The stones were slick beneath his feet, worn smooth by the passage of floodwaters, but at least they did not hurt. Above them the canyon walls closed in, stretching up two, almost three hundred feet.

Stone ground against stone as the others followed close behind him, the rocks shifting beneath their weight. To their right the river tumbled over its stony bed, roaring as it rushed down a series of cascades, making its journey through the twisting canyon. During the Spring it would rise, filling the gorge, but in the icy winter air it remained thankfully low.

Chris's gaze carried up the valley, following the sheer walls as they twisted around and out of sight. He scanned the ground ahead, picking out a trail amidst the rock-strewn ground. He was quickly adapting to the weight of his wings. His muscles surged with a newfound energy, with the joy of freedom. Behind them the mouth of the canyon was empty, but even so he picked up the pace, springing from stone to stone with hardly a pause in between. The thought of the guards and their guns drove him on. Though they were moving at a good pace, their pursuers did not have to catch them – only get them within range of their rifles.

Redoubling his efforts, Chris felt the towering granite cliffs pressing in around him. From somewhere ahead the roar of the water grew louder. Like distant thunder it drew him on, called them deeper into the mountains. Sucking in great mouthfuls of damp air, Chris raced for the first bend in the canyon.

Boulders the size of cars littered the ground. Where the canyon narrowed they clustered in groups, almost blocking their passage. They scrambled over them one by one, slipping on the damp surfaces while the others watched, waiting for their turn.

Chris's ears tingled as a voice carried up the canyon. Acting on instinct, he grabbed Liz and pulled her behind a boulder, waving for the others to follow. An instant later the shriek of bullets tore the air, followed by the sharp crack of shattered rock. Cowering behind the boulder, they watched as a boulder where they'd been standing disintegrated beneath a hail of bullets. Hot lead tore great chunks from the stone, dotting the surface of the boulder with pock-marks.

For a moment, Chris stood frozen, terrified by the sheer display of power. In his mind he saw himself caught by the bullets, saw his flesh tear and his bones shatter. Then Liz grasped him by the shoulder and shook him back to reality. He blinked, found her crystal eyes staring at him, just a few feet away, and taken by an impulse, he pulled her close.

They kissed, hard and fast, the moment filled with a desperate passion, the thrill of a chase. A second later they pulled apart and turned to face the others.

Richard raised an eyebrow, but Chris ignored him. The first bend in the canyon was close now, just a few more yards away. But the open space would leave them exposed to the guards at the base of the pass, to their unforgiving bullets.

Yet they had to move. No doubt men were already climbing towards them, growing closer with every passing minute.

"We run for it," was all Chris said before he turned and leapt from cover, unwilling to wait and see whether the others followed.

The buzz of bullets turned to a roar as he stepped into the open. Then he was racing across the open ground, stones slipping beneath his bare feet, faster than thought. With each step the shriek of bullets grew louder, the guards far below narrowing their aim. Stone chips tore his flesh as the thud of bullet impacts shook the ground beneath him. He ducked low, the hackles on his neck rising in anticipation of pain.

Then his wings were out, beating hard, driving him faster. He stumbled as he miscalculated his next jump, almost falling before recovering with a wild wave of arms. Liz bounded past, flashing him a sideways glance. But he was already up and beside her, pushing hard, lungs burning not with exhaustion, but fear. Around him he heard the gasps of the others, their desperate, unintelligible cries.

And over it all, the screech of bullets.

Then suddenly the air was clear, the cliff rising up to shield them from view. Together they drew to a stop, sucking in long mouthfuls of air, their wild eyes looking around at each other, shocked and elated, thrilled by their survival.

They did not pause for long though. They had won a respite, but they were still far from free. Ahead the canyon narrowed, the twists and turns coming closer together, and for the next thirty minutes they did not see their pursuers again. The stones grew larger around them, until only boulders remained. The giant rocks packed the gorge, the creek threading its way between them, over and under, plunging down towards the valley far below. The roar of distant water continued to grow, and the taste of the air changed, filling with moisture. In his mind, Chris pictured the stream cascading over a series of boulders, down into the canyon, and prayed it would offer them an escape.

Gathering his strength, he pressed on, drawing the others with him. The canyon floor grew steeper, winding up towards the clifftops high overhead. Their progress slowed as the way became more difficult, even backtracking where the way grew too steep, too treacherous to pass.

Striding around another bend in the canyon, Chris found his stride slowing as he took in the sight. Beside him, Liz continued her upward march, head down, eyes fixed on the ground. Around them the roar of water had turned to a deafening thunder, but it was only when he reached out and grabbed Liz by the shoulder that she looked up; that she saw where he had led them.

CHAPTER 34

CHRIS HAD NOT BEEN wrong about the waterfall. Three hundred feet above their heads, a river rushed over the edge of the cliff and out into the void. Water filled the air, whirling as the booming wind caught it, turning it to a fine mist, to a light rain that fell around them, settling on their clothes and skin. At the base of the falls, the remains of the river crashed down onto a jagged pile of rocks. From there the stream wound its way down the canyon to where the seven of them stood.

Beyond the waterfall, the canyon twisted back on itself, ending in an abrupt wall of sheer rock. A pile of rubble had accumulated against the cliff opposite the waterfall, stretching up around two hundred feet. Straggly patches of vegetation sprouted from the rubble, no doubt fed by the ready source of water.

Chris closed his eyes, feeling the spray of water on his cheeks, even where they stood some four hundred feet away. It settled in his hair and trickled down his face, until he gave an angry shake of his head and wiped it away. He clenched his fists, shivering with cold and frustration.

There was no way they could climb those cliffs, no way they could reach the top.

He had led them to a dead end, to a trap. And with the guards closing in from behind, there was nowhere left to go.

Looking at the others, he saw his despair reflected in their faces. Only Ashley seemed undaunted. She moved up beside him, her eyes travelling up the canyon, to the pile of rubble. He turned, following her gaze, straining to see through the mist. A pile of jagged boulders clustered around the top of the rubble and the cliffs above them were cracked and broken. At some point the cliffs must have given way, and now a shadow stretched up from the rubble. From the distance, there was no telling for sure, but it looked like a crack they might be able to climb.

"Let's go," Ashley flashed him a smile as she strode past, taking the lead.

Chris was glad to relinquish his position. The weight of failure hung heavy on his shoulders. The others did not speak, but he could feel the eyes of Jasmine and Richard on his back. Ahead, Ashley seemed to glide across the rocks, moving with a grace Chris wished he could match. She reached the rubble mound well before the rest of them, and started to climb.

Following her, Chris only managed a few steps before the loose gravel slipped beneath his feet. He threw out an arm, grasping at the branches of a dishevelled bush, then screamed as thorns tore the skin of his palm. Cursing, he regained his balance and released the bush, only then daring to look at his hand.

Dark marks spotted his palm; the broken thorn tips embedded deep in his flesh. Blood seeped from a dozen cuts and the skin was already turning red around the marks. He swore again, but there was little he could do now. Cradling his arm, he moved after Ashley.

The mist closed in around them as they climbed, quickly soaking them to the skin. Chris shivered as a drop of water ran down his back and caught in the clustered feathers of his wings. A tingle ran up his spine as a thought came to him then. Angela's words in the clean room rang in his mind. The feathered appendages trembled in response, as though reading his thoughts.

Fly!

Chris shook his head, casting the idea back out into the void. With the wind howling through the canyon, and the cliffs pressing close, the idea was suicide.

As they neared the top of the mound, the wind picked up speed. It howled down over the cliffs to pummel at them, tearing at their wings and threatening to send them plummeting to the rocks far below. Above, the river continued its eternal plunge over the granite cliffs, filling the air with swirling clouds of water vapour.

A cry came from above. Chris looked up in time to see Ashley slip, then threw himself to the side as a rock crashed down towards him. He shouted a warning to the others as it thumped past, but thankfully they had spread out, and it tumbled harmlessly past them.

Returning to the climb, he watched Ashley recover and continue her ascent, favouring her left hand now. But she was already drawing level with the boulders ringing the crown of the slope. Picking up his pace, Chris soon joined her at the base of the boulders. Together they turned to watch as the others joined them.

Once the seven of them had gathered on the narrow ledge, they turned to face the boulders. Here Ashley took the lead again, squeezing in between two of the boulders. The way was narrow, and the extra bulk of their wings didn't help, but Chris managed to slide his way after Ashley. Ahead, the crevice came to an end at another boulder, but Ashley was already making short work of scrambling up, using the rock on either side of her to climb.

Chris waited for her to reach the top before following. The sharp pitch of the boulders and his injured hand made it difficult to find purchase. Cursing to himself, he pressed against the rocks to wedge himself in place, and then slowly began to lift himself up.

When he reached the top, Ashley was already gone. Following her wet footprints through the boulders, his optimism began to return. If they could just wedge themselves into the crack in the cliff, they might scramble their way up in the same way they had just managed. It would be a long and difficult haul – at least a hundred feet remained to be climbed, but it was something.

He stumbled as the rocks around him gave way to open ground, and he found himself in the centre of the ring of boulders. Across from him, he found Ashley with her head pressed against the cliff, fists clenched against the sheer stone. She turned as he approached, her eyes finding his.

Chris's stomach twisted as Ashley slid down the cliff wall until she sat and covered her face with her hands. Her shoulders heaved as silent sobs shook her, and tears spilt between her fingers.

Behind her the cliff stretched up towards the sky, smooth and unmarked, the shadow they had thought was a crack no more than a change in the rock, a darker shade of granite.

They were trapped.

CHAPTER 35

LIZ PAUSED as she emerged from the boulders and found Chris and Ashley slumped against the cliff. Their faces were ashen, their eyes despondent, and she knew in that instant they were finished. Her shoulders sagged, but she moved across to Chris and placed a hand on his head. He did not look up, just stared at the barren gravel.

Crouching down, Liz pulled him to her chest. Gravel rattled as Sam appeared beside her. He squatted by Ashley, whispering softly to her, pulling her up, getting her moving again. Trapped or not, there was no time to pause, to sit and wait for death to come for them.

"I'm sorry," Chris murmured.

Liz slid her fingers through his hair and down to his chin. She turned him to face her. "This isn't your fault, Chris. You were right, this was our best chance. If we'd gone the other way, they would already have caught us. Now get up. We have to decide what to do next."

It took several tugs on Chris's arm before he gathered himself and regained his feet. By then Sam had Ashley looking more herself, though Liz suspected it was no more than a brave face. But then, that's all any of them had left now.

"So, what now?" Jasmine crossed her arms, eyes flashing as she looked around the circle. "I'm not going back."

Beside her Richard nodded.

Liz shivered, thinking of the guards creeping up the canyon towards them, of the black steel of their rifles.

No, we can't go back.

To go back now would be worse than if they'd never escaped. They had tasted freedom, rid themselves of the awful collars, breathed the fresh mountain air. And freezing though they were, with their wings drawn tight around their torsos, they were alive.

"There's nowhere left to go," Chris's voice cracked.

"Then we fight," Sam put in, his brow creased. Liz had never seen him so serious.

Around the circle, the others nodded, but Liz found herself shaking her head. Moving past them, she climbed up the closest boulder, until she was perched atop it. Looking down, she stared out over the gorge, peering through the swirling mist, seeking out their pursuers. The wind tore at her, sending her black hair flying across her face, but she ignored it.

She heard scuffling from behind her as the others climbed, but did not turn. Over the wind, she shouted back to them. "What do you think?"

Chris and the others gathered around her, and looked down over the edge.

To her surprise, Chris swallowed and retreated a step, his eyes widening. The others stood in varying states of fear, though none stood as close to the edge as Liz. To her right was the slope they had just climbed, but directly below the boulder, the gravel fell away in a sheer drop, all the way to the canyon floor two hundred feet below.

Looking down, Liz felt no fear, only a quiet resolve.

She would not go quietly back to her chains, to the cold cruelty of the doctors, to their needles and torture. She would not surrender to their bullets, to their harsh violence.

No, she would fight, she would resist, she would rage.

"You know," Ashley mused beside her. "They say birds just know. That their parents push them from the nest, and before they hit the ground, it comes to them."

"Care to go first?" Sam muttered.

Silence fell then as they stared out over the canyon, watching as the tiny specks of the guards came into view. They crawled towards them like ants, eyes searching the boulders strewn around them. But their gaze did not lift to where the seven of them stood, not yet. They were still a long way off, but they were closing quickly.

Shivering, Liz looked at the others.

They looked back, waiting.

Turning back to the edge, Liz sucked in a deep breath. Movement came from beside her as Chris stepped forward, his fingers reaching out to entwine with hers. He looked across at her, his face drained of colour. Naked fear stared from his eyes, but he smiled at her.

"Just like baby birds, right?" he tried to laugh, but it came out more as a shriek.

Liz nodded, her stomach swirling. Then she closed her eyes, and focused on the foreign appendages on her back, feeling their presence, embracing them. They were still alien to her, a violation of her body; but she needed them now, needed to embrace them as a part of her.

Concentrating, she willed them to open.

With a *crack* of unfurling feathers, the great black expanse of her wings snapped open. The others gasped, but beside her Liz sensed movement. She looked across to see the tawny brown of Chris's wings stretch out towards her own. She shivered as their wing tips met, their feathers brushing together.

Liz flashed one last look back at the others. They wore wide grins on their face now, and their eyes were alive with excitement. She grinned back, and with Chris beside her, turned to face the edge.

Together, they leapt out into the void.

CHAPTER 36

CHRIS'S STOMACH lurched up into his chest as he plunged from the edge. Below the ground raced up towards him at a terrifying speed, the jagged rocks looming large in his vision. Opening his mouth, he began to scream.

His wings gave a hard lurch, followed by a crack as they caught the air. Then he was soaring upwards, the wild wind catching in his twenty-foot wingspan, driving him up, up, up. His stomach twisted again, dropping sharply as the ground fell away. Chris let out another scream as he shot upwards and past the pale faces of his friends.

Concentrating, he focused on turning, beating his wings to counter the powerful drafts swirling around him, and risked a wave to those below. The others waved back, then with only a moment's hesitation, followed Chris and Liz off the cliff.

Chris swirled in the air, his wings twisting almost by a will of their own, and watched them plummet from the cluster of boulders. They dropped a dozen feet before their wings caught, halting their freefall and sending them hurtling back up into the sky. Broad grins split their faces, their eyes wild, their laughter echoing off the cliffs. In those briefest of moments, their hunters were forgotten, and there was only the joy of flight.

But it could not last. An ache had begun in the centre of his back, and already Chris could feel the strain in his chest and abdomen, the muscles pulling tight to keep his wings moving. With their broad expanse, there seemed to be no need for giant wing beats, but even the incremental adjustment of primary feathers and muscle was draining. Looking at the faces of the other, he could see the strain was beginning to affect them too.

The mist swirled around them, providing some cover from the guards below, or at least he hoped.

Sucking in a breath, Chris shouted across to the others, his words barely audible over the crack of air through their feathers. "We have to fly over the cliffs."

He had been studying the cliffs as the others gathered around them. They still towered above, their peaks tantalisingly out of reach. With the swirling winds doing their best to hinder them, it would take a massive effort to climb those last hundred feet. Glancing down, he searched again for the guards, and found them near the base of the rubble. They were looking up the rugged slope, but they still had not spotted them. Chris prayed they did not look up into the open air.

After all, who would have guessed they could fly?

Returning his attention to the cliffs, he willed himself upwards. Muscles strained and feathers shifted, and with a surge of elation he rose several feet. The others quickly followed him, their faces strained with concentration, their eyes fixed on the ledge above. It wasn't far, less than a hundred feet now, but the winds were shifting, fighting against them. And as they neared the top, the raging waters grew closer, soaking them through and stealing the last of the warmth from their bodies.

Still they pressed on, beating their wings in the thin air. Water accumulated in their feathers, weighing them down, but gritting his teeth Chris pressed on. His stomach tightened as muscles he had never used stretched and twisted, driving his wings forward, sending him upwards.

Bit by bit, the top of the cliffs drew closer.

When they were still thirty feet away, Chris risked a glance down, and swore.

The guards were staring up at them, pointing, their eyes wide and mouths open in shock. But already one was dropping to his knee, and the others quickly followed suit. Rifles were raised to shoulders and a gun barrel flashed. Almost three hundred feet above, the seven of them presented an easy target.

Without thinking, Chris's wings twisted, sending him whirling sideways, even as he screamed at the others.

"Look out!"

Then the air was alive with the screech of bullets.

The others scattered like a flock of doves, flying outwards in all directions, though they strained to continue upwards. Up towards the clifftops, towards safety.

Straining for breath, Chris drove himself on, though every inch of his body was screaming. Threads of terror wrapped their way around him, but somehow he found the strength to hold on. His wings worked by instinct now, alive with the rush of desperation, driven by the need to escape.

Abruptly he found himself in clear air. One instant the whiz of bullets and howling wind was all around him, then it was gone. Looking down, he realised he had made it, that he had crossed the threshold of the cliffs. The canyon had disappeared from view, dropping away as he shot over the icy ground a few feet below, still tracking the stream upwards.

Glancing back, he watched Sam shoot up over the lip of the cliff and then dive towards the ground, quickly followed by Jasmine and Richard. They evened out about thirty feet from the ground and raced towards where Chris was pulling up and twisting to meet them. They wore wide grins on their faces, though their cheeks were red and their breath billowed out in clouds of vapour.

Chris looked past them, holding his breath, waiting for Ashley and Liz and the girl.

They appeared one by one, Liz, the girl, and finally, rising laboriously into sight, Ashley. Liz and the girl swept down towards them, but Ashley was struggling to maintain her height. Her wings were barely moving now, and her face was turning purple. She still hovered over the lip of the cliff, drifting slowly towards them, driving by sheer determination now.

Her eyes closed with sudden relief as she reached the clear air. Straightening out, her wings spread wide to catch the gentler breeze. A smile warmed her face as she looked across at them.

Then her smile faltered, her eyes widening as a shot echoed up from below. A red stain flowered in her chest and blood sprayed the air. Without a sound, Ashley's wings folded, and she plummeted to the icy ground.

Ashley lay in a tangled mess of limbs and feathers and wings, her flesh torn and broken, her face buried in snow. The only signs she lived came from the slow rise and fall of her back, the low gurgling coming from her chest. She coughed, half-rolling to reveal her battered face. Blood seeped between her lips in a slow trickle, staining the snow beneath her.

She didn't move as they drew closer. Her eyes were closed, and there was little chance she could be conscious after the fall. Chris was shocked she was even alive; though he wasn't sure that was a blessing for her, or a curse. Her wings lay at awkward angles around her, and when he glanced at her legs he had to look away.

The bullet had taken her in the back and passed straight through her. Somehow it had missed her heart, but with the blood bubbling from her mouth, it appeared to have found a lung.

Another groan rattled from Ashley's chest, tearing at Chris's heart. He crossed the last of the distance between them and crouched beside her. Tears built in his eyes, but angrily he wiped them away. Reaching out, he grasped Ashley's hand and gave it a gentle squeeze.

"Ashley," he whispered as the others gathered around them. "Ashley, it's okay, we're here."

Ashley. Brave, bold, elegant. When he'd first laid eyes on her, he'd thought her fragile, a sheltered city girl incapable of standing up for herself. She had put those misconceptions to rest with her first words. And time and time again since. She had proven stronger than any of them, her will unquenchable.

And now she lay here on the side of a mountain, her blood staining the frozen earth, and there was nothing any of them could do to help her.

She was dying.

Stones crunched as Sam crouched beside him. Tears streamed down the larger boy's face. Stretching out a hand, he wiped the blood from Ashley's lips, as though the simple act might wake her, might bring her back to them. A sob tore from his chest as a fresh bubble of blood rose between her lips and burst.

He reached for her, as though to draw her into his arms, and then stopped. He crouched there with one arm outstretch, torn between his desperation to help her, and the fear he would only hurt her further.

The others stood around them in silence, each lost in their own thoughts.

Long minutes dragged by as they watched her struggle, her every breath a desperate fight for survival. They had time to spare now, though in truth all thought of escape had vanished. On the harsh mountainside, they sat by their friend and watched her life slip away.

But as minutes ticked towards an hour, Ashley still clung to life. Her body was torn and broken, her life-blood staining the snow red, but still she breathed, still she fought on.

Finally Chris knew they could wait no longer. Sucking in a breath, he stood. Tears stung his eyes as Liz joined him, sliding an arm beneath his shoulder. He looked at the others, saw the indecision in even Jasmine and Richard's eyes. They could not stand there waiting for her to die. And yet, they could not abandon her, could not let her last moments on this earth pass alone on this harsh mountainside.

He looked at the others, hating the question in their eyes. They wanted him to make a decision, though he was not quite sure when he'd become the leader. It felt strange, especially given Richard and Jasmine's animosity. But there was no time to debate it now.

"We can carry her," Chris whispered at last.

"No," Sam croaked, surprising him. The young man looked up at him, his eyes red with tears, and shook his head. "No, you can't bring her with you. She'll only slow you down."

"We can't leave her," Liz said.

Sam closed his eyes, a shudder going through him. "I know," he breathed.

Chris stared at him, a tightness growing in his stomach. "What do you want to do, Sam?"

"Go, Chris," Sam looked up at them, resolution shining from his eyes. "Go. Take the others with you. Leave, fly away, be free. I'll look after her," his voice broke as he finished, but there was iron in his words.

Looking down at Sam, Chris wondered at his courage. He opened his mouth to argue, to convince him to come with them, that they could carry her, keep her comfortable until…

"Maybe they can save her…" Sam finished.

With those five words, Chris realised they would never change Sam's mind. He meant to sacrifice himself for Ashley. He would give away his freedom, his life if there was the slightest chance she might live. Looking at her, Chris tried and failed to summon the same hope. Between the bullet and the fall, there was little left of the graceful girl he had known.

But still she fought on, her iron will unyielding. And thinking of the miracles the facility had performed on them, he wondered if Sam might be right.

At last he nodded. In his arms, Liz began to tremble, but he pulled her tight before she tried to argue further. She glanced up at him, anger burning in her eyes, but he only shook his head.

This was Sam's decision to make. His alone.

Jasmine and Richard glanced at each other, their

shoulders slumped. Whatever their history with Ashley and Sam, Chris doubted they had ever wished for this. Perhaps they would even miss his comedic presence.

"Good luck, Sam," Chris said, swallowing hard.

Sam nodded and then turned back to Ashley. With the utmost care, he slid his hands under her back and lifted her into his arms. She gave a tiny groan as she left the ground, seeming to shrink beside Sam's massive frame. Her head lifted, her eyelids fluttering, before she nestled her head into the crook of Sam's arm and grew still.

Gently, Jasmine and Richard helped tuck the shattered mess of Ashley's wings into Sam's arms. Then they stood in silence as Sam moved back towards the cliffs. His copper wings slowly spread as he walked towards the edge, his back straight, his gaze fixed straight ahead. He did not look back as he reached the edge. Without hesitating, stepped out into open air.

They stood for a moment after he had disappeared, waiting for the gunfire, praying he would reach the ground safely. But they did not go to the edge. They did not watch.

Chris didn't know about the others, but he could not bear to see Sam return to his chains.

Finally Chris wiped the tears from his eyes and faced the others. They stood shivering in the cold mountain air, their eyes red, their faces pale. Even so, they faced him, waiting.

But there was only one thing left for them to do now.

Fly.

ENJOYED THIS BOOK?

Then follow Aaron for a free short story:

www.aaronhodges.co.nz/newsletter-signup/

Phase One: Complete.
The Project Continues in: <u>RENEGADES</u>

The change has begun. A new species is rising. Our world will never be the same…

Chris and Liz have survived the Praegressus Project, but that was just the beginning. The vile experiments have altered their physiology – granting them super-human strength and speed. Oh, and wings. Now, lost in the Californian mountains, they must master their newfound abilities and return to civilisation. But they are not alone in the wilderness. In the chaos of their escape, the *Chead* were also freed. Deadly, barely human, they stalk the darkness, hunting…

AFTERWORD

Hello, and thank you for reading Rebirth! This was my first foray into the genre, so I'm very interested to know your thoughts! Please remember to leave a review over on your vender of choice!

FOLLOW AARON HODGES:
And receive a free short story…

Newsletter:
http://www.aaronhodges.co.nz/newsletter-signup/

Facebook:
www.facebook.com/Aaron-Hodges-669480156486208/

Bookbub:
www.bookbub.com/authors/aaron-hodges

59615187R00151

Made in the USA
San Bernardino, CA
05 December 2017